MONTANA M

Welcome to Big Sky Country, home of the Montana Mavericks! Where free-spirited men and women discover love on the range.

THE ANNIVERSARY GIFT

The mayor of Bronco and his wife have invited the whole town to help celebrate their thirtieth anniversary, but when the pearl necklace the mayor bought his wife goes missing at the party, it sets off a chain of events that brings together some of Bronco's most unexpected couples. Call it coincidence, call it fate—or call it what it is: the power of true love to win over the hardest cowboy hearts!

Lights, camera...*action*! Celeste Montgomery is used to life in the spotlight, so she thinks she can handle playing Ross Burris's wife for a month. It's a mutually beneficial deal—she will save her network reporting job, and the flirty rodeo rider will redeem his reputation in town. But their "foolproof" plan hits a snag when their hearts unexpectedly get involved...

Dear Reader,

One rodeo bad boy in need of an image makeover. One sports reporter looking to hold on to her job. What harm could a one-month marriage of convenience do?

Rodeo cowboy Ross Burris is charming, sexy and is rumored to have a different woman in every town. But when television sports journalist Celeste Montgomery is assigned to Bronco, Montana, to interview a rodeo performer, a sport she knows nothing about, Ross sees an opportunity to help her to secure her position at her Chicago-based network—and to dispel the negative social media comments about his reputation as a "Rodeo Romeo"—if they marry under the pretense they were secretly dating.

Celeste agrees to elope with Ross because the stories she plans to submit to her network on her so-called secret lover should counter the negative comments, while reporting on a superstar celebrity athlete is certain to increase the station's ratings and hopefully earn her a promotion.

They agree to the mutually beneficial arrangement—with no perks of any kind—and at the end of thirty days of living together as husband and wife in name only, they are free to divorce each other. Ross and Celeste become consummate actors as they fool everyone in Bronco into believing their story. But with each passing day, they are tested because there is nothing in their agreement about not falling in love—for real.

I hope you will enjoy *The Maverick's Thirty-Day Marriage* as much as I enjoyed writing about this dynamic couple who will keep you turning the pages as they make every effort to turn thirty days into forever.

Happy reading,

Rochelle Alers

THE MAVERICK'S THIRTY-DAY MARRIAGE

ROCHELLE ALERS

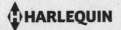
HARLEQUIN

Special thanks and acknowledgment are given to
Rochelle Alers for her contribution to
the Montana Mavericks: The Anniversary Gift miniseries.

ISBN-13: 978-1-335-59477-8

The Maverick's Thirty-Day Marriage

Copyright © 2024 by Harlequin Enterprises ULC

Harlequin Enterprises ULC
22 Adelaide St. West, 41st Floor
Toronto, Ontario M5H 4E3, Canada
www.Harlequin.com

Printed in Lithuania

Since 1988, nationally bestselling author **Rochelle Alers** has written more than eighty books and short stories. She has earned numerous honors, including the Zora Neale Hurston Award, the Vivian Stephens Award for Excellence in Romance Writing and a Career Achievement Award from *RT Book Reviews*. She is a member of Zeta Phi Beta Sorority, Inc., Iota Theta Zeta Chapter. A full-time writer, she lives in a charming hamlet on Long Island. Rochelle can be contacted through her website, rochellealers.org.

Books by Rochelle Alers

Harlequin Special Edition

Montana Mavericks: The Anniversary Gift

The Maverick's Thirty-Day Marriage

Bainbridge House

A New Foundation
Christmas at the Château

Montana Mavericks: Brothers & Broncos

Thankful for the Maverick

Furever Yours

The Bookshop Rescue

Wickham Falls Weddings

Home to Wickham Falls
Her Wickham Falls SEAL
The Sheriff of Wickham Falls
Dealmaker, Heartbreaker

Visit the Author Profile page
at Harlequin.com for more titles.

Chapter One

Ross Burris was leading the stallion out of the stable to join the other grazing horses when he saw the stray dog coming in his direction. He'd left fresh water in the stable for him. It was a ritual that had begun a week before when Ross found the small brown and tan poodle-terrier-mix puppy asleep next to the horse stalls. But whenever he attempted to touch him, the dog scampered off, which prompted Ross to call him Scamp.

He wasn't certain where the canine had come from or whether he had an owner. After drinking water, Scamp would disappear and then return in the evening to find some food waiting for him. It was the least Ross could do; he'd always had a soft spot for animals.

Once he'd earned enough prize money as a bronc rider Ross had bought the property with a modest house, barn, a stable with enough stalls for six horses, two outbuildings, and enough grazing land for a small herd. He'd also purchased an abandoned building closer to town in Bronco Valley. Once it was renovated, he planned to establish an after-school enrichment program where volunteers could assist students with their homework, lessons, and test prep. But, that only would become a reality once he retired from the rodeo.

It was the beginning of May, and in another seven weeks he would return to the rodeo circuit, but meanwhile he wanted to enjoy springtime in Montana. The brilliant sun in a cloudless sky indicated another hotter than usual day. Taking a handker-chief from the pocket of his jeans, he pushed back his Stetson and wiped his forehead. Then he began mucking, washing, and hosing the stalls before he climbed the ladder to the loft for a bale of hay.

He'd come to enjoy the physical ranch work because it not only kept him in peak physical condition but afforded him time away from competing. However, Ross wasn't going to begrudge a sport that had been responsible for him earning enough money for a comfortable lifestyle.

And then there was being in the spotlight as one of the younger brothers of Geoff Burris, known as the Tiger Woods of rodeo. As one of the most famous Black rodeo riders in the country, Geoff had elevated the Burris name so that the hype went into overdrive whenever they competed. For Ross though, since moving onto the ranch, he had come to look forward to spending more time at home than on the road. When he'd men-tioned going into semi-retirement, Geoff and Jack had teased him that at twenty-six he was too young to sit on his porch and stare at the sunset like a grandpa. However, what they didn't know was that he was more like his brother Mike who was in medical school. Except that Ross's focus, like their parents, was education. Their mother taught kindergarten; their father was a high school principal and basketball coach.

The sun was still high in the sky when Ross returned to the house and checked his cell phone. He had a voicemail message from the Bronco Convention Center's new market-ing director asking him to see her about a promotion proj-ect. Curious, he set up a meeting for later that afternoon and got cleaned up.

Two hours later, after Ross parked his Silverado at the convention center, he found Rylee Parker in her office. He knocked softly on the open door and her head popped up. She smiled when she saw him.

"Please come in, Ross. And thank you for coming."

Ross took a seat opposite her and returned her smile. He pointed to the diamond ring on her left hand. "Congratulations on your engagement." Rylee was now engaged to local rancher Shep Dalton.

Rylee shyly lowered her blue eyes. "Thank you." A beat passed, then she said, "I wanted to talk to you about being interviewed by a television reporter doing a piece on rodeo performers. Her boss wanted her to get an exclusive with Geoff, but because he's out of the country I thought you would step in for him."

Surprised, Ross leaned back in his chair. He had thought Chuck Carter, the manager of the convention center, had come up with another event, like the Mistletoe Rodeo and Bronco Summer Family Rodeo, which would include the Burris and Hawkins rodeo families. His brother Jack had married Audrey Hawkins and his brother Mike was engaged to Corinne Hawkins. He also did not want to agree to the interview when he knew his days and years as a rodeo performer were winding down.

He shook his head. "I don't know about this, Rylee." Ross was hesitant to agree to the interview because he didn't want to give up spending time at the ranch.

She picked up a folder and handed it to him. "Before you turn me down, please look at this. The reporter works for the Chicago affiliate of a major television station and her credentials are impeccable. And I'm certain a little more publicity can only elevate your family's profile."

Ross thought Rylee was coming on a little too strong with her pitch, but the instant he opened the press kit and saw the black-and-white headshot of the reporter he suddenly had a change of mind. Celeste Montgomery wasn't smiling, yet there was a barely perceptible parting of her lips that drew his rapt attention. Everything about the woman radiated confidence. He flipped through the pages, pretending to be interested, while the image of the journalist's beautiful face was imprinted on his brain.

"She really needs this interview, Ross."

"Why?"

Rylee tilted her head. "If you agree, I'm certain she'll explain everything to you."

Ross closed the folder and set it on the desk. The near-pleading tone in Rylee's voice aroused his curiosity. Just why did Celeste Montgomery need this interview? "Okay. Tell Ms. Montgomery that I'll meet her tomorrow at one at DJ's Deluxe. I'll be waiting for her at the bar."

Rylee laced her fingers together in a prayerful gesture. "Thank you, Ross."

Pushing to his feet, he stood and nodded. "You're welcome." He was curious as to why Celeste had accepted the assignment to do a story on Black rodeo performers. He was also curious if she would look as good in person as she had in her photo, and there was only one way to find out, and it would be to meet her the following day.

I suppose one Burris is better than no Burris.

That was what Celeste Montgomery continued to tell herself as she walked into the upscale barbecue restaurant in Bronco Heights. When Rylee had called to tell her Ross Burris was willing to meet her, she'd immediately researched him. And what she'd discovered had given her pause. Unlike his brothers Geoff, Jack, and Mike, Ross had come to be known as a Rodeo Romeo. The consensus was he had a different woman in every town, and his reputation as a love 'em and leave 'em guy had relegated him to *bad boy* territory.

Celeste wasn't sure of Ross's romantic exploits, but she *was* certain her boss had sent her to Montana to get rid of her. Well, Dean Johnson might have it in for her, but Celeste was determined to prove she could manage any assignment.

Dean had wanted her to get an exclusive with Geoff Burris, but with him out of the country on an extended vacation with his fiancée, she settled on the next best thing. Another Burris brother.

Celeste pulled back her shoulders when she walked into DJ's Deluxe and saw Ross Burris sitting at the bar. It was no wonder women flocked to him like bees to flowers. The man was gorgeous. She didn't know why, but Celeste thought he would've worn a plaid shirt, jeans, and boots and not the snap-button white shirt, black suede jacket, tailored slacks, and shiny black boots. So much for her believing the stereotype of the quintessential cowboy. He picked up a black Stetson off a stool and met her as she extended her right hand.

"Thank you for agreeing to meet me, Mr. Burris."

"No problem, Ms. Montgomery."

Celeste felt the calluses on his palm and a shiver of awareness shot up her arm when she looked up into the large deep brown eyes that she found mesmerizing. She struggled to pull her gaze away and her eyes lit on his mouth outlined by a trimmed mustache and goatee. "Please, call me Celeste."

Ross inclined his head as he released her hand. "I will only if you call me Ross."

Celeste smiled at the same time she drew in an audible breath. She didn't know why, but meeting Ross Burris had taken her breath away. "Then, Ross it is."

"Do you mind if we conduct your interview over lunch?"

"Of course not." Celeste hadn't had anything other than a cup of coffee earlier that morning because she spent hours on her laptop scrolling through posts on social media while jotting down notes. And she was glad Ross had suggested eating at DJ's Deluxe because she loved barbecue.

* * *

Ross seated Celeste, then rounded the table to sit opposite her. He knew it was impolite to stare, but he couldn't pull his gaze away from Celeste as he focused on her long black straightened hair and expressive brown eyes and delicate features in a flawless khaki-brown complexion. Everything about her screamed big-city elegance with her black tailored pantsuit, designer heels, and matching handbag. Pearl studs in her ears and the strand on her slender neck completed her professional look.

"Would you like something to drink before we order?" he asked as he lowered his eyes.

"Yes. I'd like a sparkling water."

Ross signaled for a waiter and put in their beverage requests. He waited for her to peruse the menu and when the waiter returned with their drinks, they both placed their orders.

Lifting his glass of craft beer, he touched his glass to hers. "Work is good, provided you do not forget to live."

Celeste peered at him through her lashes. "Did you make that up?"

Ross shook his head, smiling. "No. That's a Bantu proverb."

She went still. "You know about the Bantu people?"

He looked surprised. "Surely you researched me." At her nod, he added, "And what did you uncover?"

A beat passed while Celeste took a sip of water. "That you don't have the best reputation when it comes to women."

Ross shook his head. "You can't believe everything you read."

"Oh, it's like that," she said, as she gave him a look that he interpreted as disbelief. "You're denying what's been posted on social media, that you're a love 'em and leave 'em guy?"

"Vehemently. Now, do I look like the type to take advantage of a woman?"

"I don't know, Ross, because I don't know you."

He grinned across the table. "Are you saying you would like to get to know me?"

Celeste's jaw dropped before she quickly recovered. There was no way she was going to permit herself to be drawn in by this cowboy oozing sexual magnetism. She had worked much too hard to be taken in by the charm he flaunted like a badge of honor.

"If you mean getting to know you well enough for you to grant me an interview, then yes."

"If, and I say *if* I agree to the interview, then I want final approval on whatever you submit to your network."

"Are you saying you don't want me to question you about a recent incident involving a Texas woman and a video of your breakup?"

"That's exactly what I'm saying."

It was obvious from his expression that he didn't like her mentioning his reputation with women and she decided to press the issue. "What about the other women who posted similar comments about you?"

His back straightened. "Do you plan to interview me about the rodeo or my personal life?"

"But isn't your personal life tied to the rodeo?"

"No. What I do as a bronc rider has nothing to do with what I do when I'm not competing. And as a professional journalist I'm certain you don't believe everything you read on the internet."

"Yes, you're right about that. But as a journalist I must have the facts."

Ross took a drink, then his eyes met hers, and she felt as if they saw straight through her. "Let me ask you, Celeste. What do you know about the rodeo?"

"Absolutely nothing."

"I don't understand. Why have you been assigned to cover a sport you know absolutely nothing about?"

Celeste knew she had to be straightforward with Ross for him to agree to be interviewed. "I had no input when it came to this assignment."

A slight frown appeared between Ross's eyes. "Something's not adding up. You claim you're clueless when it comes to knowing about the rodeo, yet you're assigned to interview one of the sport's more popular bronc riders?"

Celeste lowered her eyes. She knew it was time to become completely open with Ross. "It's my boss."

Ross leaned over the table. "What about him?"

"I used to think he doesn't like women. Then I realized he just doesn't like *me*, and lately he's been making my life a living hell. He's setting me up to fail when assigning me to a project I know nothing about because he wants me to quit, but I refuse to give him that satisfaction. He sent me to Montana because for him it's out of sight, out of mind." She paused. "It's unprofessional of me to dump this on you, but you need to know why I really need this interview."

"There's no need to apologize, Celeste. I'm certain if we put our heads together, we can kill two birds with one stone."

Her brows creased as she gave him an inquiring look. "Two birds?"

"You can help me repair my bad boy image while I can help you keep your job."

Now she was intrigued. What exactly was he planning in that handsome head of his? "How?"

"It's something big, but I'm not certain whether you'll be able to manage it."

Celeste, aware of Ross's reputation as a player, hoped he wasn't about to try and mess with her head. She'd had enough of that with her last boyfriend. "I won't know what it is until you tell me."

"Marry me."

Ross watched as she held a napkin over her mouth to stifle the laughter she was helpless to control. She was still laughing when the server set their orders on the table.

"What made you come up with something as ludicrous as that?" she asked, once the man walked away.

Celeste may have thought it was ludicrous, but for Ross it wasn't. "I know you've read things about me on social media, but I need to explain the last one that has generated overwhelmingly negative comments about me."

"Tell me about it."

"I met that woman in Texas, and we shared dinner twice because I found her interesting, but nothing beyond that. She thought we were a couple and when I told her we weren't she turned on me."

"She claimed you were a couple after two dates?"

Ross nodded. "Yes. Unfortunately, it was played out in a restaurant where someone videotaped her rant and posted it. What followed was an onslaught of postings that basically said Ross Burris is a dog who thinks that commitment is a four-letter word."

"What about relationships?" Celeste asked.

"I haven't had many serious relationships because I haven't wanted one."

"You don't want a serious relationship, yet you want me to marry you?"

Ross wanted to tell Celeste that he wasn't ready for marriage, but circumstances beyond his control dictated that he had to do what was necessary to make his dream of opening the student center a reality. While on the rodeo circuit, he'd spent his free time taking online courses at graduate school and now that he was ready to embark on the second phase of his life, negative comments on social media were threatening to derail all he'd sacrificed to achieve.

Ross nodded again as he stared at his steak burger covered with a balsamic glaze and topped with bacon jam. "If we marry, then I know things will change. What's being posted bothers me because I know, and my family knows, none of it's true."

Celeste pointed to his plate. "You need to start eating before your food gets cold."

After Ross took a bite, he told Celeste about his future plans. "I want to start a nonprofit after-school learning center for kids in Bronco Valley. But those plans may be impacted because of the negative comments about my character. I'm giving the rodeo another four years before I stop competing full-time."

With wide eyes, Celeste asked, "You're retiring?"

"Not completely. I still plan to compete but part-time."

Celeste was more confused than ever. Ross wanted her to marry him—a stranger—but how could that help him, or better yet benefit her? "This sounds much too confusing for me, Ross."

He reached across the table, then held her hand. "We'll have to become consummate actors and appear to have fallen madly in love with each other. It'll have to look like you're so special that I couldn't imagine my life without you, and I had to propose marriage. That this is the reason I didn't become involved with other women because I was in love with Celeste Montgomery. I'm certain this backstory will surpass you interviewing my brother."

Had he been kicked in the head by a bull one time too many? "Nobody is going to believe that, Ross. That we were seeing each other secretly."

Ross increased his hold on her hand. "Would you believe

that you're the first woman I've ever felt an instantaneous connection to? When Rylee showed me your press kit with your photo, I knew I wanted to meet you."

Celeste was helpless to ignore the tingling sensations that made her more than aware of her physical reaction to Ross Burris. That told her his charm wasn't lost on her and that she had to be careful not to be taken in by it. Neither could she ignore his intention to set up a nonprofit for schoolchildren. Maybe he was right and the online negative comments about his treatment of women were wrong. Still…

"I don't know, Ross. This all just seems so…ridiculous. I—" Her words were cut off when her cell phone dinged a familiar ringtone. "Excuse me, but I must answer this. It's my boss. Hello, Dean."

"Did you get the interview?"

Celeste closed her eyes and held the phone away from her ear. She didn't know why he had to shout whenever he spoke to her. "Not yet. But I'm working on it."

"You gave me that excuse more than a week ago. How long is it going to take for you to get an interview with Burris? I'm warning you that if you don't get the story then I'll assign it to someone else who is a lot more qualified."

She opened her eyes and saw Ross staring at her. "I said I am working on it." She'd stressed each word. Ross took out his cell phone, his fingers moving quickly, and then turned it for her to see what he'd typed. "Wait a minute, Dean," she said when reading what Ross had put on his phone.

Tell him you'll have an even bigger story than the interview with Geoff. If you'll marry me.

"I said that I'm working on it because I have an even bigger story than the one with Geoff Burris, and it has to do with one of his brothers." She hoped she sounded convincing.

"What is it?"

"I can't tell you now, but I'm certain you'll like it."

"Okay, Celeste. Whatever you're working on better be something that will boost ratings."

She didn't want to believe Dean was talking about boosting ratings while she was trying to keep her job. "Oh, I'm certain it will," she said, while praying that she wasn't about to cross the line and compromise her career.

But when she thought about interviewing Geoff Burris or marrying his so-called bad boy brother, Ross, there was no doubt the latter would generate a social media frenzy. And knowing ratings-hungry Dean Johnson, he would eat up every word.

"Did he buy it?" Ross asked once she ended the call.

Celeste nodded, smiling. "I think he did."

"So, what's it going to be, Celeste? Are we going to get married?"

In that instant Celeste felt as if she were on a precipice. Either she had to remain rooted to the spot or jump off into the unknown. And the unknown was becoming Mrs. Ross Burris. She'd promised Dean she would deliver something that would boost ratings, and she knew she had to follow through on the promise or be reassigned, or even possibly fired. Dean knew she liked being a TV sports reporter, and her future included becoming a sports announcer.

She drew in a ragged breath and let it out, slowly. She could hardly believe it when she said the word, "Yes."

Ross smiled and she returned it with one of her own, hoping she appeared more confident than she felt at that moment.

"Now it's time to get started. Where are you staying?"

"I'm at the Heights Hotel."

"I suggest you check out. I'll come by later this afternoon to bring you to my place, and we'll go over the plans for our whirlwind courtship and marriage."

"You want me to sleep at your house?"

"Of course. It makes sense if we've been dating and planning to marry."

Celeste could not ignore the pinpricks of heat flooding her face. She was a twenty-eight-year-old woman who'd had one meaningful relationship, and she didn't want Ross to believe she wouldn't be able to hold her own in their marriage of convenience.

"I'll be packed and ready when you get there," she said, as the waiter brought the bill.

She hated that Ross handed the server his credit card before she could. It made her feel like this was a date, which it wasn't. It was a simple arrangement. To repair his less than favorable reputation, while at the same time get her an exclusive on one of rodeo's Black superstars.

Ross settled the check and walked her to her rental car in the parking lot. He took a step toward her, bringing them less than a foot apart. "I'll pick you up at four. You can either turn in your rental car or leave it at the hotel. I have an extra vehicle you can use while you're here."

Celeste nodded. "Okay, I'll be in the lobby."

He took another step, angled his head, and brushed his mouth over hers. "Later, bae."

Celeste froze. She hadn't expected him to kiss her, but realized he was attempting to make their relationship appear real to anyone who saw them. When she noticed people staring at them, Celeste put an arm around his neck and, going on tiptoe, breathed a kiss under his ear.

"Later, my love," she whispered.

She knew she'd shocked Ross when he stared at her in stunned silence. If it was his intent to play a game, then he didn't know that she was more than up to the task. She'd interviewed more than her share of flirty professional athletes in her career, and she'd learned how to deal with them.

She waited for Ross to open the door to her vehicle, and then slipped in behind the wheel. She drove out of the parking lot, leaving him standing in the same spot. Something told Celeste that Ross Burris was used to controlling everything and all situations. But not this time. He wanted a fake wife to enhance his image—but she needed a story that was certain to blow up the internet.

Chapter Two

Celeste was waiting in the hotel lobby with her luggage when Ross walked in. Even though she had checked out, she'd paid to leave her rental car in the hotel's parking lot. Smiling, she stood as he approached her. He'd changed into jeans and a white T-shirt that blatantly displayed an incredibly toned upper body and muscled biceps. She noticed women turning to stare at him, before exchanging nods. It was obvious they approved of her future fake husband.

During the drive back to the hotel Celeste had gone through mental calisthenics about what she was about to embark upon. How was she going to pretend that she and Ross Burris were secretly dating each other, had fallen in love, and were now planning to marry?

Celeste felt her confidence vacillate slightly when she met Ross's eyes and, in that instant, she said a silent prayer that she would be able to hold her own with this rodeo celebrity. *Suck it up, Celeste, because you can do this.* She told herself that she had no choice but to see the charade to its conclusion and secure approval from her boss. If Dean Johnson wanted the staged melodrama of reality television, then Celeste would bring it like fireworks lighting up the skies on the Fourth of July.

Ross dipped his head and kissed Celeste's cheek when it was her mouth he'd wanted to kiss. The mere brushing of his mouth over hers in the restaurant parking lot earlier that afternoon was to make it look good for anyone noticing them, because he knew it would generate talk if Ross Burris was seen kissing a woman in public. It wasn't as though he'd never done that before with any other woman, but it was different with Celeste. He had to convince himself they had to make their so-called secret relationship appear to be the real thing. And what he'd planned to propose would make them actors in award-winning roles. Celeste would get her story and he would salvage what was left of his less than positive image.

"Are you ready?" he asked, reaching for the handle of her suitcase.

"Yes."

Ross rested his free hand at the small of her back as he led her to his vehicle. He felt the warmth of her body through the white silk blouse she'd paired with a slim-fitting black pencil skirt. Celeste had said she was ready, but Ross still wasn't certain whether he was. But he knew he had to get ready if they were to pull off the ruse that they were truly madly in love with each other.

Ross had no idea where the marriage idea had come from even before he'd noticed Celeste's agonized expression as she'd attempted to explain to her boisterous, overbearing boss who was talking loud enough for Ross to hear him; it was as if the idea had just materialized. It was a way to change his damaged reputation and for Celeste to let her boss know she was not going down without a hell of a fight. What Ross hadn't known was whether Celeste would go along with his scheme, but instinct told him she was a fighter. That if she left the network, it would be her decision and not because she'd been bullied.

When they reached his vehicle and he opened the passenger door to the pickup, it was obvious Celeste was going to have a problem getting into his vehicle, because she was wearing a skirt and heels. His hands circled her waist as he lifted her effortlessly and settled her on the leather seat. Ross certainly hoped she had packed jeans and a pair of boots in that suitcase of hers.

A slight smile parted her lips as she nodded. "Thank you."

Ross inclined his head. "You're welcome." He rounded the truck and slipped behind the wheel. "Once we get to the ranch, we can hash out the conditions of our marriage, because we've got to get everything in motion."

"You said we'd get our…relationship going immediately, but just how soon do you plan for us to marry?" Celeste asked.

"I'd like for us to marry in Vegas and be back in Bronco before the weekend."

She turned to stare at him. "That soon?"

Ross met her stunned gaze. "Yes. I realize that gives us only a few days, but there's no need to wait, Celeste. Your boss is complaining that you're taking too long to complete your assignment and we must move fast for him to get off your back. Besides, May is sweeps month, right?" He didn't wait for her reply. "Meanwhile we have to appear to be madly in love for my family to believe that we decided to elope because we didn't want a long engagement."

Celeste didn't know why, but she hadn't thought of the impact of the pretend marriage on both their families. "Do you think you'll be able to fool your family, Ross?"

"That all depends on you."

"Why me?" Celeste asked.

Ross checked his mirror and accelerated onto a road leading to his house in Bronco Valley. "I'm the one with the reputation for dating a lot of women, Celeste, so my parents will be relieved to know that I'm now ready to settle down with one woman."

Celeste shook her head. It was one thing to fool the public, but she wanted to draw the line when it came to family. "Not only will we be lying to your family but also mine." She paused, suddenly feeling a bit sick.

"What we must do, Celeste, is make everyone believe what we have is real. Should we write up a contract outlining the details?"

She shook her head. "That's not necessary."

"I agree," he said. "Everything should go smoothly because there will be no sexual favors and exchange of money between us."

Celeste concurred with that provision. She knew becoming physically involved with her temporary husband would spell disaster—at least for her. And she had to remain in control of her emotions because she knew it would be too easy to get caught up in the sensual force field Ross Burris gave off whenever they shared the same space.

"Okay," she said in agreement. "Once we're married, I'll begin filing a series of stories highlighting our affair."

"While you do that, I'll use my rodeo connections to raise your profile in the industry. Once we accomplish whatever we need to do we can quietly separate, but only if your position with the network is secure, or if you can get a better offer. I figure that'll take a month, so plan on being married for the month of May."

"What happens after that?" she asked.

Ross gave her a quick glance. "After what?"

"After the charade is over. I don't intend to live with or remain married to a man I don't love."

"You can be the one to file for divorce. I'll appear emotionally upset that you don't want to stay married, and I'll tell everyone that I was willing to let you go so you can advance in your career, because that's something you wouldn't be able to do living in Bronco."

"Are you sure you can pull off acting like the brokenhearted Rodeo Romeo?"

"We'll have to wait and see, won't we, Celeste?"

"If you're able to pull that off, then you shouldn't have a problem convincing everyone that you're nothing like what has been posted about you on social media."

"That's what I'm hoping."

"So, you're serious about not letting your family in on our secret."

"Very serious," Ross said. "If my parents or brothers even suspect what we have is a sham, then we won't be able to pull it off. As soon as I get to the house, I'm going to reserve a flight so we can get married in Las Vegas. Meanwhile, tomorrow we can shop for rings and wedding attire."

"Can't we do that in Vegas?"

He shook his head. "We have to shop in Bronco so people can see that Ross Burris is turning in his bachelor card to marry a woman he's been secretly dating."

"You have an answer for everything, don't you, Ross?" she said accusingly.

"I've thought about this, Celeste, and if we can pull this off, then it's a win-win for both of us. Our futures will depend on how well we can execute what you call a charade."

Yes, a charade where I must pretend that I love a man I'd only met earlier today. How good an actress do I think I am?

Even though Celeste agonized over what she'd agreed to, she knew Ross was on to something. She needed a newsworthy story that would save her job; he needed people to change their perception of him so he could open his nonprofit. The reasons were certainly valid. But could they pull it off? There was so much she didn't know about her soon-to-be husband.

"Before I tell you about my family, we should concoct a story about where we first met."

"Have you ever been to Fort Worth, Texas?" Ross asked.

"Yes. Why?"

"When were you there?"

"I went to Dallas in January to interview a backup quarterback for the Cowboys, and then I stopped to visit a friend from college who'd moved to Fort Worth after she'd married her husband."

"That's perfect. I participated in the Fort Worth Stock Show & Rodeo where I competed in the Cowboys of Color Rodeo. This year it ran from January twelfth to February fourth. We can tell everyone that we met in Fort Worth and that's when we felt an instant connection."

She could hardly believe how fortuitous that timing was.

"Do you have your own place in Chicago?" Ross asked.

"Yes. I have a townhome in a suburb called Ashburn."

"Do you live alone?"

"Yes."

"Good."

"Why would you say that?" Celeste asked.

"Because that means I could have come to see you without anyone knowing. Tell me about your family. Have you always lived in Chicago?"

"No. I was born and raised in Buffalo, New York. I went to college in Chicago and after graduating I got a position at the network as an intern. My parents still live in Buffalo. My father is a dentist, and my mother is an elementary school principal."

Ross smiled. "We have something in common because my father is also a principal. What about siblings?"

"I have older twin brothers. Rodney is a pharmacist and Reggie is a lawyer."

"Do they live in Buffalo?"

Celeste shook her head. "No. Rodney's married, and he lives in Orlando, Florida, with his wife and two girls. Reggie is a JAG officer in the navy, and his wife is also in the military. She's a doctor. My family will be as shocked as yours once I tell them I eloped with a man I was dating on the down-low."

* * *

Ross grimaced when Celeste said *down-low*. She'd made it sound as if they were engaged in something sleazy. Even though he had concocted a scenario that would prove beneficial to both their futures he'd hoped there wouldn't be any collateral damage if he and Celeste stuck to the rules. And despite being physically attracted to her, Ross had told himself that sleeping with his wife was not an option.

"Do you think your folks will be disappointed once we separate?" he asked.

"I don't know, Ross," Celeste said, as she stared out the side window. "Once my brothers were married, my mother said she was looking forward to becoming the mother of the bride."

"It is different with my mother because she has four sons."

"Your brother Jack is married, and I read that Mike is engaged to Corinne Hawkins, plus Geoff has that long engagement to Stephanie Brandt. So that just leaves you to tie the knot."

When competing, he rarely spent time with the other contestants because he'd had to keep up with his coursework. And when he did take time to see a woman it was usually to take her to dinner or a concert. However, he was always available to the press for interviews because as a Burris he belonged to one of the country's most popular Black rodeo families.

While he was touted professionally, it was his personal life that had taken a hit. And if he could turn back the clock, he never would've agreed to share dinner with the woman who'd thought nothing of making a scene. He was certain things would've turned out differently if he'd met Celeste instead of his narcissistic date.

"What are you thinking about?" he asked Celeste when she fell silent.

"I never would've imagined I would marry in Vegas with

an Elvis impersonator as the witness instead of my friends and family."

"We won't be married long, so you can file for an annulment rather than a divorce."

Ross's hands tightened on the Silverado's steering wheel when he registered the regret in Celeste's voice, and in that instant, he chided himself for setting her up for disappointment. She deserved better than marrying a stranger in a resort city without the benefit of her loved ones in attendance. However, under the circumstances, it couldn't be helped.

Ross realized even if he hadn't gotten Celeste to agree to marry him, that eventually the Texas incident might blow over. But the internet was forever, and the hateful stories posted there would never go away, available for any celebrity gossip hunter. He wasn't willing to risk that. For Celeste, though, the situation was worse. Her boss clearly had it in for her. Or perhaps he was a chauvinist who thought women belonged in the kitchen and not in a locker room. Either way, it was clear he'd sent her to Montana to cover a sport she knew absolutely nothing about. And Ross aimed to fix that.

Celeste wanted to tell Ross that it didn't matter whether their marriage ended in divorce or an annulment. She just wanted to give Dean what he wanted and then return to Chicago, safe in her job and hopefully on track for a promotion. She'd come to work for the network as an intern, and after three years she was now in line to become the network's weekend permanent sports correspondent. And those who oversaw the affiliate were aware that the station's ratings always went up whenever she covered a sporting event.

"An annulment and divorce are one and the same to me, Ross. Once it's finalized, we will be free to marry someone we love and want to spend the rest of our lives with."

"And hopefully it won't take you long to find that person who will love you as much as you love him."

Celeste stared at Ross's profile as he concentrated on the road. Marriage was not at the top of her wish list, because she'd planned to travel to major cities on three of the seven continents before she celebrated her thirty-fifth birthday.

"I wish the same for you, Ross."

A swollen silence filled the interior of the pickup, each lost in their own thoughts, until Ross said, "What made you decide to become a sports reporter?"

Celeste smiled. "It's in my DNA. My dad's grandfather played in the Negro Leagues. And my father and brothers are addicted to sports. There was never a time when I was growing up that the television wasn't tuned to either baseball, basketball, or football. And forget about the Olympics. But I never remember watching the rodeo."

Ross gave her a quick glance. "If I'm going to watch sports, then it's rodeo and then baseball and basketball. I watched Ken Burns's baseball documentary, and I was astounded by the talent of the Black baseball players. Those players were phenomenal. So many of them were superior to those in the major leagues, and if they'd been allowed to play alongside them, I'm certain they would've put them to shame."

"How much do you know about the Negro Leagues?"

"Enough. When we get to my house, I'll show you a collection of books written about them."

"So, the cowboy reads," Celeste said teasingly.

Ross chuckled. "Growing up with my parents, who are both educators, our home was filled with books on every subject. My brother Mike and I would challenge each other as to how many books we could read in a year."

Intrigued by the story, Celeste asked, "Who won?"

"Mike did, only because we hadn't established from the onset whether they had to be picture or chapter books or comics."

"How old were you when you started this?"

"I was nine and Mike was eight."

"The fact that you were reading must have really impressed your parents."

"My mother couldn't have been happier."

"What was her reaction when all of her sons decided they wanted a career in rodeo?"

"I'm certain she wasn't pleased because of the risks of being injured, but even if she didn't approve, she's always supported us." He clicked on the turn signal and made a left at the next intersection. "My place is coming up soon. After you settle in, I'd like to take you around the property and introduce you to my horses." He gave her a quick glance. "Do you ride?"

"Does sitting on a pony and being led around in an enclosure at a county fair count as riding?"

Throwing back his head, Ross laughed.

"It's not that funny, Ross. I was only five."

He sobered quickly. "I'm sorry for laughing. Am I forgiven?"

Celeste crossed her arms. "I'll have to think about it."

"How long will that take?"

"I don't know, Ross. I'm still deciding."

"Don't take too long because we're here."

Lowering her arms, Celeste stared at the two-story stone and wood house with a wraparound second-floor balcony and an attached three-car garage. It was where she would live for the next month as Mrs. Ross Burris. "It's beautiful." The two words had slipped out unbidden.

Ross shut off the engine and draped his right arm over the back of Celeste's headrest. "I haven't lived here long, so there are still a few changes I'd like to make to some of the rooms."

"How long have you lived here?"

"It'll be a year in December." He got out and ran around to open her door. "I'll help you down."

Celeste felt pinpricks of heat in her face. When she'd put on the skirt that afternoon, she didn't know she'd be riding in a pickup. Summoning all her grace, she swung her legs around, but not before she saw Ross's gaze on her bare thighs where the skirt had ridden up.

Wrapping her arms around his neck, she closed her eyes when her breasts contacted his chest as he held her effortlessly off the ground. His arms tightened around her waist. She wanted to tell him to let her go, but it was as if her vocal cords were paralyzed. She pressed her face against the column of Ross's strong neck. His warmth, the lingering scent of a woodsy masculine cologne on his skin, and the strength in his arms were both frightening and thrilling at the same time.

Celeste and Ross had agreed there would be no sex during their marriage of convenience, but what she was feeling frightened her because at that moment it was exactly what she wanted and needed. It was close to two years since the breakup with her long-time boyfriend and she had sworn off men, telling herself she didn't want or need them in her life. But it was different with Ross Burris, because whenever he stared at her Celeste experienced something she hadn't felt in an exceptionally long time. Desire.

"Please put me down," she whispered in his ear.

Seconds ticked before Ross lowered her to the ground. "I hope you packed something less fancy in your luggage because you need to save your heels and tight skirts for when you go back to Chicago. Jeans and boots are the norm here."

Celeste looked up at him through her lashes. There was just a hint of a smile playing at the corners of his mouth, bringing her gaze to linger there. "I have a few outfits that are less *chic*," she said, stressing the word. "I did pack some leggings, sweats, and running shoes, and one pair of jeans, but it looks as if I'll have to go shopping."

"Once we come back from Vegas, I'll take you to Cimarron Rose. It's a popular boutique owned by Evy Roberts, and I'm certain you'll be able to find something you'd like there."

"Can't we shop there tomorrow when we go for rings and wedding attire?"

Ross shrugged. "If we have enough time. But don't forget you have to find a wedding gown."

Celeste blinked slowly. "You think I need to wear the traditional gown and veil?"

He nodded. "We gotta make this look good, bae."

"You're really into this, aren't you?" Celeste asked.

Ross nodded again. "And I need for you to play along with me. That way in the end we'll both come out winners."

That was the second time Ross implied she might not be able to make people believe that she loved him enough to become his wife. And it tweaked her. "Oh, you think I can't step up and play the adoring wife when we're in public, Ross?"

"I don't know, Celeste."

"You don't know, but you're about to find out, because whenever I accept a challenge, I have no intention of failing."

"That's my girl."

"No, Ross. I'm your woman and soon to be your wife. Please try and remember that."

"Well, damn," Ross said under his breath. "I guess you told me."

Celeste patted his chest. "I need to change before you show me around." She waited for Ross to take her suitcase out of the pickup and walked with him to the house.

She didn't know what to expect, but it wasn't the exposed timber trusses, wood paneling, and a dramatically painted gable ceiling in the living room. Large picture windows, bisected with sash work, offered expansive views of mountains off in the distance. Her gaze was drawn to the wood-burning fireplace, and she imagined sitting in front of a warm fire during the winter months while snow blanketed the outdoors with nature's pristine whiteness.

"Your home is beautiful," she said reverently.

"*Our* home," Ross whispered in her ear. "You must think of this house as ours."

Turning her head, she smiled at him. "Our home is beautiful."

Ross's eyelids lowered. "And it's yours to decorate however you wish."

"But I'm only going to be here a month, Ross."

"Only you and I know that. I'm certain my brothers will occasionally stop by and no doubt comment on the changes my wife made to turn my bachelor pad into a home."

"You trust me to decorate your—I mean *our* home?"

Ross dipped his head and kissed her forehead. "What I trust you with is our secret."

"You didn't answer my question, Ross. Do you trust me to make changes to this house?"

"Yes." Reaching for her hand, he steered her to the staircase. "I'll show you to your bedroom. After you change, I'll take you to see the horses. Once they're stabled, we can go into town for dinner."

"How's your fridge?" At his puzzled look, she added, "Is there anything I can put together for dinner?"

"You don't want to go out to eat?"

Celeste shook her head. She didn't want to tell Ross that she wanted to stay in and get used to sleeping under the same roof with a man who was a stranger. That she needed the time to emotionally fortify herself before going out the next day to shop for wedding rings and attire.

"Not tonight," she said.

"I can make honey-glazed salmon with oven-roasted garlic potatoes."

"You cook?"

Attractive lines fanned out around Ross's eyes when he smiled. "Yes, I cook." He paused. "Do you cook?"

Celeste inclined her head. "Yes. And quite well."

"This will be our first test."

"And what's that?" she asked.

Ross winked at her. "Cooking together as a couple."

A couple who within days would go from strangers to husband and wife.

Celeste didn't have to wonder if she'd have considered dating Ross if they'd met under different circumstances. She knew the answer was no.

Even if the woman in Texas hadn't gone off publicly about Ross unceremoniously dumping her, what Celeste had read about him being labeled a Rodeo Romeo was enough to turn her off, because in her last relationship there were rumors of her boyfriend seeing other women, but she hadn't believed it until she was able to witness it herself when she'd gone to their favorite restaurant with one of her coworkers to find him hugged up with another woman. They were so into each other that it had taken him a while to realize she was standing only feet away from their table.

DeAndre had attempted to play it off and introduce his date as a college friend, but Celeste refused to accept the lie. She'd joined her coworkers at their table and deleted him from her contacts, while blocking his numbers. He'd called the station for a week and when she refused to answer his calls, he'd finally gotten the hint that it was over.

She had given him more than a year of her life, while it was to be different with Ross. Their liaison had a one-month expiration date.

Short.

Without drama.

And no regrets.

Chapter Three

"**Y**ou're giving me the master bedroom?" Celeste asked, when Ross set the suitcase near a wall of closets. "Where will you sleep?"

"The bedroom across the hall."

"But… But what…" Her words trailed off into silence.

Ross took a step, bringing him closer to her. "I'm giving you the master because if we're married then it would make sense that your clothes would be in here with mine. Every night I'll get my clothes for the next morning and leave them in the other bedroom. Both bedrooms have ensuite baths, so we won't have a problem walking in on each other. I get up early to take care of the horses, so you can sleep in as late as you want."

"How early do you get up?"

"I'm usually up between five and six. Why?"

"Because I'd like to have breakfast ready for you."

A wide grin spread over Ross's features. "So, you're going to become a dutiful wife and prepare breakfast for her husband?"

"Don't get ahead of yourself, Ross. It's only going to be for a month. After that you can go back to your regular routine."

"What if I get used to one month, and then want another?"

"One month, Ross Burris. That's all you're going to get from me. I have a job and a life in Chicago, and I'm counting down the days when I can return."

Her statement got him thinking. Was pretending to be married to him so off-putting that Celeste couldn't wait for the charade to end? He wanted to tell her that he hadn't married yet because he'd felt that he wasn't ready to become a husband and someday a father.

However, he did have a wonderful role model in Benjamin Burris. His father called his wife of more than three decades his queen and treated Jeanne as one. And whenever Ross saw Geoff and Stephanie, Jack with Audrey, and now Mike with Corinne, it was obvious that the Burris brothers loved the women they'd chosen to share their lives and futures with.

He'd researched Celeste online and discovered there was nothing documented about her personal life. Instinct told him that she wasn't currently in a relationship, otherwise she wouldn't have agreed to a marriage of convenience. A very public marriage of convenience.

"Why do I get the impression that you're identifying with a prisoner marking off the days on a calendar before her release from jail?"

Celeste lowered her eyes before she gave him a long, penetrating stare. "I'm sorry if I gave you that impression, Ross, but all of this is new to me. I'll sort it out." As if she was talking to herself, she said, "We'll be together for a month, and I promise to wait a couple of weeks after I leave before I announce the news that we're going our separate ways. That my working in Chicago and your involvement with the rodeo circuit is not advantageous for a stable marriage."

Ross couldn't help but wonder if Celeste believed the gossip about his being a playboy on the rodeo circuit. He couldn't get into Celeste's head to know what she was thinking but, in that instant, he told himself that all he could do was be himself—the Ross Burris that his close friends and family knew. And that he would treat her with the respect he'd shown every woman.

He forced a smile he didn't quite feel. "I'll be in the kitchen getting the ingredients for dinner. You can come down whenever you're ready."

Celeste had hoped she hadn't come on too strong, but she wanted Ross to know that they were playing a game—a game she hoped resulted in them both coming out as winners. What she did not want to acknowledge was that there was something about him that made her question herself whenever they shared the same space. No, it was *everything* about him, including his gorgeous face, magnificent body, and his characteristic charm that made him a magnet pulling at her when she least expected. She hadn't spent twenty-four hours with him, and she had seen firsthand why women flocked to him. And she'd just discovered she was no exception.

Celeste knew she had to be careful—incredibly careful not to feel things for her temporary husband.

The bedroom Ross had chosen for her was twice as large as the one in her town house, with French doors that opened out onto the balcony with magnificent views of the rural landscape. It was so different from when she peered out her bedroom window that overlooked the residents' parking lot.

Celeste opened the suitcase and took out a pair of leggings, running shoes, and a long-sleeved T-shirt. She styled her hair in a ponytail and went downstairs. She found Ross in the kitchen/family room that was in the center of the house and was bisected by an L-shaped kitchen counter.

His back was to her, and it gave her the opportunity to admire the way his jeans hugged his slim hips and long legs. Light from overhead pendants shimmered on his black cropped hair. Celeste cleared her throat and he turned to look at her. "I'm ready to take the tour."

Ross nodded. "As soon as I wash my hands and put on another pair of boots, I'll be with you."

His mentioning changing his boots instinctually told Celeste that Ross Burris was a neat freak. The wood floors were so shiny she could almost see her reflection in them. "You don't wear shoes in the house?"

After rinsing his hands in one of the double stainless-steel sinks, Ross wiped them on a towel. "I have a pair of boots I only wear when I'm working in the stable. Whenever I come in, I leave them in the mudroom."

Celeste stared at her running shoes. Now she knew why Ross had mentioned that she should purchase a pair of boots.

"I never wear my shoes inside my home," she told him.

"Do you go barefoot?"

"No. I leave my shoes in the entry and wear socks with grippers."

"Like those they give patients in hospitals?"

Celeste smiled. "Yes, but mine are more fashionable. I like them to be fun and colorful. And what do you know about hospital socks?" she asked him, then paused. "How many times did you have to be taken to a hospital because you were injured when competing?"

"No comment," Ross said, as he cupped her elbow and led her out of the kitchen to the rear of the house.

She gave him a sidelong glance. "And because you're refusing to answer I suspect it has been more than a few times."

"It was just because the doctors wanted to rule out any serious injury."

"What about the nonserious injuries?" Her knowledge of the rodeo was limited, but Celeste knew that even the famous Burris brothers were no match for a two-thousand-pound bull or a half-ton horse falling on them.

"I was bucked off a horse that kicked me in the head. Even though it hurt like hell, I kept telling everyone that I was all right. But I wasn't all right. I wound up in the hospital with a concussion. They kept me for a couple of days, and once I was discharged, I took the doctor's advice and didn't compete for the next three months. So that's why I'm familiar with hospital socks."

Celeste followed Ross as he led the way through a laundry room and into the mudroom where he stopped to pull on a pair of mud-covered boots before they left the house.

She felt a cool breeze on her face as they headed outside. The temperature had dropped dramatically from earlier that afternoon. "This weather reminds me of Chicago. There's an old saying that if you don't like the weather, wait five minutes and it will change."

"It's been unseasonably warm these past few days. Our average spring temperature is usually in the midforties, but lately it's been in the seventies. If you're cold, we can go back and get a jacket."

Smiling, Celeste shook her head. "Nah, I'm good." Growing up in Buffalo and then moving to Chicago she was more than familiar with double-digit snowfalls and bone-chilling below-freezing temperatures.

Ross gave Celeste a quick glance. "Are you sure?"

"Very sure."

He'd struggled not to stare at Celeste in the body-hugging leggings. She was slim but shapely. What he did not want to admit to himself was that she was perfect. Everything about Celeste radiated big-city sophistication, and he wondered if they'd met under a separate set of circumstances whether she would have been interested in dating a rodeo cowboy. Or would a long-distance relationship—casual or otherwise—have been a deal breaker?

Ross was more than aware that even if he'd been in a committed relationship, his life as a rodeo rider wasn't always conducive to stability in a relationship, yet knew it was a personal choice because there were plenty of rodeo cowboys who had settled down happily, and that included his brothers. And then there was another factor. Despite the deep affection he'd witnessed between his parents and his brothers and their significant others, Ross was cynical when it came to true love. It was all right for others, but not for him. At least not at this time in his life. However, now he had to become an actor, and play the role of loving boyfriend and fiancé. Once he'd suggested to Celeste they marry, he'd contemplated announcing the news without going through a ceremony, but then realized that it would be too easy for someone to uncover the deception. To make it real they had to make it legal.

"We're going to have to take the pickup to the meadow, where the horses are grazing."

Once they were in the vehicle, Celeste looked around. "What's in that building?" She pointed to a small structure about a hundred feet behind the house.

"Nothing. I still haven't decided what I want to do with it."

"If it were mine, I'd convert it into a workout space or a home office."

Ross nodded. "That is a possibility. But first it would have to be equipped with plumbing and wiring." He winked at her. "And I thank you for the idea."

Celeste gave him a warm smile. "You're welcome. How large is your property?"

"Approximately twenty-two acres."

"Did you plan on buying property this big?"

"No," Ross admitted. "I wanted to purchase another property with a smaller house and enough land for a couple of horses, but that changed once the Realtor showed me this place and the prior owners decided to meet my price."

Ross knew the house with four bedrooms and five bathrooms was much too large for a bachelor, but it was the size of the property and what the owners were willing to give up for the selling price that made him reconsider. The owners hadn't wanted to transport their prized horses to their new home overseas and when they offered to give him the stallion and the two pregnant mares, that had sealed the deal for Ross. Both mares had given birth in March and he'd had Bronco's veterinarian, Felix Sanchez, check out the new foals and he had declared them both healthy.

Staring out the side window, Celeste watched as the landscape changed as Ross maneuvered over an unpaved road, driving past a stable until he stopped near a fenced-in area where a magnificent black stallion grazed with two near-white mares. She smiled when seeing two tiny foals lying beside their mothers. It was apparent the stallion had sired the foals because one was all black and the other white with black markings.

"Oh, Ross! They're beautiful."

"Yes, they are." He told her how he'd acquired them.

"Their babies are just adorable."

"The stallion is Commander, and the two mares are Blizzard and Belle. I named the colt Traveler because he likes to run, and the filly is Domino because of her black and white markings."

"Do you plan to also become a horse breeder?" Celeste questioned.

Ross shook his head. "No. The mares are young, so once they foal again, I plan to have them sterilized. Daniel Dubois breeds horses. He's married to Brittany Brandt. She's Stephanie's sister, who happens to be engaged to my brother Geoff."

Celeste laughed. "It looks as if I'm going to need a scorecard to distinguish who's who in your extended family."

"Not to worry, bae. I'll give you a play-by-play once everyone gets together."

"You'll need to give me a play-by-play before I meet them, Ross. If we're supposed to be seeing each other since January, then I should know something about your family other than their names."

"Don't worry," Ross repeated, "I'll make certain you'll come through okay. I don't have to know that much about your family other than their names and what they do, because I'll tell everyone that we were secretly dating, and you didn't want your family to know that we were involved with each other."

"But what if they ask why I didn't tell them, Ross?"

"Maybe you can say something like you come from a bougie family, and they wouldn't approve of your marrying a rodeo rider."

"Hey! My family's isn't bougie."

"They're bougie enough. Your father is a dentist, and your mother is a principal, while one of your brothers is a pharmacist and the other a lawyer. And don't forget that your sister-in-law is a doctor."

"What about your folks? Your parents are educators and one of your brothers is in medical school. And you, Mister Rodeo Romeo, have managed to earn two degrees in education, so I'll thank you not to call my family bougie as if it is a dreadful thing."

"Okay, let me rephrase, then. You can say that they wouldn't approve of you becoming involved with someone who makes a living riding bucking horses or roping bulls. That I would be more acceptable if I'd played in the major leagues, given the fact that one of your ancestors did play in the Negro Leagues."

"That sounds better, Ross."

Reaching over, Ross tugged on her ponytail. "Thanks for your approval. Now it's time I take the horses back to the stable. You can stay in the truck until we get there."

Celeste watched through the windshield as Ross got out of the truck and picked up a rope from behind the driver's seat. He opened the gate to the corral and whistled sharply until Commander trotted over to him. After looping the rope over the stallion's neck, he led him to the rear of the pickup. As if on cue, the mares and their foals followed. He tied the rope to the hitch on the pickup and then got back in and drove slowly to the stable.

She got out of the pickup and stood in the doorway as Ross brushed each horse before giving Commander, Blizzard, and Belle feedbags filled with oats and then water before leading them into their stalls. Traveler and Domino were content to suckle their mothers as they joined them in their respective stalls. Celeste jumped slightly when she spotted movement out of the side of her eye, then realized it was a dog. The brown and tan puppy trotted in and sat in a corner.

"I didn't know you had a dog," she said to Ross.

"I don't," he said, as he took a bowl off a shelf and filled it with dry dog food. "He comes around in the morning for water and at night for food. I call him Scamp because he scampers away before I can touch him."

Celeste walked over to the tiny dog and patted his head as he looked up at her with large brown eyes. She scrunched up her nose. "You need a bath. Ross, can we take him back to the house and clean him up?"

Ross halted filling the bowl. "I can't believe he let you touch him."

"That's because he knows I like dogs."

"I like them, too, but he won't let me touch him."

"Can I take him back to the house and give him a bath?" Celeste asked again.

"You want to take him home?"

"Yes. If he comes around every day, then it's because he's looking for a home."

"This stable is his home. He sleeps here every night."

"Okay, but why can't we give him a bath?"

Ross groaned aloud. "Celeste, you can't go around picking up strays."

"He's not a stray, Ross. It's obvious he's lost, and he needs someone to take care of him. And that's what you've been doing if you've been giving him food and water." A slight frown furrowed her forehead. "Who's going to take care of the horses while we are in Vegas?"

"I pay someone to look after them whenever I'm away."

"Will he look after Scamp?"

"Yes, Celeste," he drawled. "He's well aware that he must take care of Scamp."

She rolled her eyes at him. "You didn't have to say it like that. I promise Scamp goes back to the stable once he's cleaned up."

Ross threw up both hands. "Okay. But don't get too attached to him because he may belong to someone."

"Don't worry, my love. If someone does claim him, I promise not to make a scene."

"My love?"

She blew him an air kiss. "Yes. I'm practicing."

"Why do I get the impression that you're going to do a lot of practicing whenever you intend to get over on me?"

Celeste didn't want to believe that she was that transparent—that she and Ross hadn't spent twenty-four hours together, yet he had seen through her ploy to bring the puppy home. "You're wrong, Ross."

He took two steps, bringing them less than a foot apart. "I don't think so," he said, as he looked at her, their eyes locking, before he turned away.

Celeste hadn't realized she'd been holding her breath until she tried to inhale, her heart beating a runaway rhythm as if she'd run a long, grueling race. "You're wrong," she repeated once she recovered. Without warning, Ross turned to face her, his hands going around her upper arms as he pulled her close to his body. His head came down as if in slow motion before he covered her mouth with his in what was more a caress than a kiss.

Celeste felt as if she were drowning, sinking lower and lower with the pleasurable sensations that weakened her knees until she clutched at Ross's T-shirt to maintain her balance. The kiss ended, and Celeste realized Ross was as turned on as she was when he buried his face against her neck, his uneven breathing reverberating in her ear.

"What are you doing, Ross?"

"I'm practicing, my love."

She released Ross's shirt and took a step back to put distance between them. The silent voice in Celeste's head shouted that it wasn't going to work. There was no way she could pretend she was in love with Ross without the pretense possibly becoming a reality. He hadn't touched her intimately, yet she was unable to ignore the delicious waves of pleasure rippling through her and the need to feel him inside her.

She told herself it was because it had been almost two years since she'd shared a body with a man—a deceitful man who didn't deserve the time and the passion she'd given him. It was only day one and Celeste prayed it would get easier, and not harder, to resist the man with whom she'd pledged the next month of her life.

"As soon as Scamp finishes eating, we should get him back to the house," she managed to say in a raspy voice she hardly recognized.

Ross smiled, the gesture not reaching his large mahogany eyes as he cradled her chin and brushed his thumb over her cheekbone. "As you wish, *my love*."

Celeste resisted the urge to thumb her nose at him as she'd done so often as a child whenever her brothers did something to her, until her mother had begun grounding her for what she said was an unladylike habit. And for Sandra Montgomery, the ultimate affront to her dignity was to be embarrassed by her daughter's unladylike behavior.

Celeste watched the puppy empty the dish of food, then lap up the water in the other one. Then she picked him up and cradled him to her chest, hoping he wasn't covered with fleas or ticks. She cooed at the pup the whole ride back to the house, though not a word of conversation passed between her and Ross.

Ross smiled at Celeste across the dining room table. She'd washed the dog, showered, and changed her clothes by the time he set dinner on the table. "Scamp looks like a different dog."

Celeste returned his smile. "A spa treatment will do it every time." She touched a napkin to the corners of her mouth. "I think I've changed my mind about cooking for you."

Ross angled his head. "Why?"

"Because you're a better cook than I am. The salmon is the best I've ever eaten."

"You wouldn't have said that a couple of months ago. When I first moved here, I got so tired of eating beef every night. But every time I made fish, whether it was baked, fried, or grilled, it wasn't fit for human consumption. Then I finally got a cookbook and was able to achieve a modicum of success."

"I'd say you achieved perfection."

"Does this mean I have to cook every night?"

Resting her elbow on the table, Celeste cupped her chin with her hand. "Not every night. I'm certain we'll be able to work out a schedule that's equitable. I forgot to ask, but do you have a housekeeper?"

Ross nodded. "I've hired a woman who comes in twice a week to do laundry and light cleaning when I'm not competing."

"Give her the month off, Ross. I'll do the cleaning."

Ross shook his head. "There's no way I'm going to allow you to clean this house."

"Either that or word will get out that we're not sleeping together when she washes two sets of bed linens not one."

Ross groaned. "I didn't think about that."

"Well, I did. So, I suggest you let her know that you won't need her services for the next thirty days."

Ross came around the table and leaned over Celeste to kiss her hair. "Thank you for thinking ahead. I'll call her now. Then I'm going to take Scamp back to the stable."

Celeste peered up at him over her shoulder. As a journalist she'd learned to think creatively, and check and recheck every fact, before submitting a report to her producer. Once again, her skills came in handy. "I'll clean up the kitchen while you're gone."

"Thanks, bae."

She smiled. "There's no need to thank me, Ross. We're a couple."

"I'm certain you'll remind me whenever I forget."

Ross was talking about forgetting when Celeste doubted whether she would ever forget him as long as she lived.

Chapter Four

As promised, Celeste was preparing breakfast when Ross returned to the house minutes before seven.

She'd been pleasantly surprised when she found fresh and frozen fruit and vegetables, containers of egg whites, lean meats, and fish in his refrigerator. It was obvious he was very health conscious, and the result was an incredible toned body that had her giving him furtive glances. And she also had begun fantasizing what it would be like for them to sleep together like a normal married couple. Her musing would remain just that—a fantasy—because she and Ross had agreed to live in the same house as roommates, and despite her physical attraction, Celeste knew making love with him would sabotage her assignment. She'd told herself once she gave Dean and the network what she knew would boost ratings and solidify her position at the network she would leave her husband and everything she'd shared with him in Bronco, Montana, behind.

She also had admitted to herself that she was looking forward to becoming a temporary wife for one of rodeo's more popular bronc riders. She had even thought of the publicity pitch for their wedding: *Rodeo's Romeo Finds His Juliet.*

Ross had showered and changed when she set a cup of coffee and a spinach egg white omelet at his place setting. He dug in as soon as she sat and moaned. "Wow! This is delicious.

I could get used to this," he said, smiling. "Do you realize that you're spoiling me?"

"This is day two of thirty, so we still have a lot of time to spoil each other."

In between bites Ross said, "After we finish breakfast, we need to go into town to shop."

"Where are we going first?" Celeste asked.

"Beaumont and Rossi's Fine Jewels for rings. It shouldn't take that long for us to find something you like, then I'll drop you off at Ever After for your wedding gown, while I go to The Dashing Cattleman for my tuxedo. Hopefully, we won't have to wait more than a day for alterations, because we're scheduled to fly into Vegas Wednesday morning. We'll check into one of the hotels on the strip, get a license, and then find a wedding chapel for the ceremony. We'll spend a couple of days in Vegas on an abbreviated honeymoon, then come back to Bronco by the weekend."

Celeste nodded. It was obvious after she'd agreed to marry Ross that he hadn't hesitated to make plans for their wedding. "I researched Vegas weddings and discovered that we can fill out a marriage license application online."

"Good. Then we can save time and do that today."

"We need to hire someone to film everything," Celeste said, "because I'm going to need footage to send to the network. He can tape us when I interview you before we leave Vegas and upload it to Dean for him to include in a timeslot that would generate the most interest." She had made prior arrangements with Rylee to use someone from the convention center's audio-visual department to videotape her interviews in Bronco.

"There's no doubt *that* should boost ratings during sweeps."

"It's what I'm hoping, Ross. And I'll make certain the interview will help to dispel some of the negative talk about you."

Celeste knew she and Ross were only playing a game, but when she thought about marrying him there was the possibility that it would be the only time that she would become a bride. DeAndre had dashed that dream. He had pledged his undying love for her, saying when the time was right, they'd get engaged, but after a while Celeste realized the time was never right because not only was he seeing her but other women. And now when she looked back, she realized the time would never have been right because they had been going in different directions. He complained incessantly that he never saw enough of her because of her traveling for work.

"What time is our flight?"

"Eleven thirty."

Celeste had better get ready. And fast. *Suck it up, girl. In two days, you're going be known as the wife of rodeo superstar Ross Burris.*

"See anything you like?" Ross stood next to Celeste as she peered at the diamond rings in the display case at Beaumont and Rossi's Fine Jewels. She could feel him gauging her reaction when the salesperson showed her each ring on the tray.

Celeste looked at him. "They're all beautiful. I can't decide. Why don't you select one for me?"

Ross had suggested purchasing a diamond engagement ring and matching wedding band, but Celeste told him that given the timing, one band would be better. They'd decided on an eternity band.

"How about this one?" Mr. Mason, the salesperson, asked as he held up a platinum ring covered entirely with brilliant blue-white diamonds.

Leaning closer, Ross whispered in her ear. "That would look perfect on your finger."

Celeste stared at Ross as if he'd taken leave of his senses. She didn't have to be a certified gemologist to ascertain the carat weight of the diamonds. Two carats. At least.

Mr. Mason took a quick look at the attached tag. "You're in

luck because it's your size. The diamonds set in platinum are near flawless and weigh 3.75 carats."

Ross took the ring and slipped it on Celeste's left hand. It was a perfect fit. "How does it feel?"

She wiggled her fingers. "It's very comfortable."

"If my fiancée likes it, then I'll take it. And I'd also like a band."

Celeste was still surprised Ross wanted a wedding band. Then again, a ring would make their marriage even more profound to his friends and family.

"Ross Burris, you sly devil. You finally did it, didn't you? You managed to stand still long enough for a woman to rope you in."

Celeste stared at the attractive young woman with a dirty-blond ponytail. A nametag with the jewelry store's logo was pinned on her jacket lapel. Tiffany.

Gilbert Mason frowned at her and a rush of color suffused Tiffany's face. "Sorry, Mr. Mason."

Ross rested a hand at the small of Celeste's back. "Sweetheart, I'd like you to meet Tiffany Brooks. Tiffany and I were in the same high school graduating class. Tiffany, this is my fiancée, Celeste Montgomery."

Tiffany's hazel eyes narrowed slightly. "Haven't we met before?"

"I don't think so," Celeste said. She was certain she had never met the woman.

"It is possible that I've seen you before because you look familiar?" Tiffany asked. She closed her eyes for several seconds, then opened them. "Now I know. I remember watching a YouTube video where you were interviewing a football player who had just announced his engagement to one of my favorite social media influencers."

Celeste smiled. "I do work in television."

"I knew it! I can't wait to tell everyone that I met a TV celebrity." She pointed to Celeste's ring. "When's the big day?"

"Soon," Celeste said.

"Good for you." Tiffany glanced at the wall clock. "It's time for my shift, so I have to clock in. Nice meeting you, Celeste. Congratulations again, Ross."

He nodded. "Thanks, Tiffany."

A half hour later, Celeste and Ross left the jewelry store with their rings. When Mr. Mason totaled the purchases, Ross's only reaction was to reach into his pocket and take out a credit card. Celeste could not understand why he was willing to spend so much money on a sham of a marriage. The man was clearly desperate to reverse his reputation with women.

"Are you ready for the chatter?" Ross said, when they sat in the pickup. "Because I'm willing to bet that before the sun sets everyone in Bronco will be talking about Ross Burris going to Beaumont and Rossi's Fine Jewels to buy a woman a ring."

"But isn't that we want? For talk to get out that rodeo superstar Ross Burris has stopped tomcatting and is ready to settle down with a wife?"

Ross frowned. "Wouldn't womanizing sound better than tomcatting, Celeste?"

"Tomcatting is more low-down than womanizing. And what has been posted on social media about you equates to tomcatting."

"Let's hope we won't have to wait long for folks to post some more favorable comments about me."

As he drove away, Celeste asked, "Have you decided on a tuxedo?"

"A Western style, in blue or gray."

Celeste smiled. "Okay, cowboy."

"You approve?"

"Of course, I approve, Ross. You must represent your profession."

Ross parked in front of the bridal shop, got out, and helped Celeste down. Putting his arms around her waist, he pulled her close and kissed her mouth. "See you later, bae."

Celeste smiled. "Later, sweets."

He nuzzled her ear, laughing softly. "It looks as if we're getting good at this boyfriend and girlfriend thing," he whispered.

Anchoring her arms under his shoulders, Celeste rested her head on his chest. "Practice makes perfect." Even though she didn't like public displays of affection, she knew others had to believe that she and Ross were so hopelessly in love that they couldn't wait to marry.

Funny, though, that kissing him seemed to be getting easier each time…

Ross waited for Celeste to enter the bridal shop, when he heard a familiar voice call his name as he opened the door to the pickup. He turned to see Garrett Abernathy walking toward him.

"Hi, Garrett. What's up?" he asked, extending his hand.

"That's what I should be asking you," countered Garrett Abernathy as he shook his hand.

Garrett had become an unofficial member of the Burris extended family because he was engaged to Brynn Hawkins, whose sister Audrey had married Jack. Her sister Corrinne was now engaged to his brother Mike. The Abernathys were one of the wealthiest families in Bronco, second only to the Taylors.

Garrett angled his head. "Is there something going on with the young woman you were kissing that you don't want to talk about?"

"There's not much to talk about except that it's taken a while for me to find someone I want to settle down with. Celeste works as a sports reporter."

"Where did you two meet?" Garrett asked.

"We met earlier in the year in Texas. We hit it off right away. We managed to see each other whenever she wasn't on assignment, and I was in between competing." Ross couldn't believe the lie had rolled off his tongue so smoothly. He almost believed it himself.

"Good for you. I know how that is because when I met Brynn for the first time, I knew then she was special."

Ross had heard that Garrett had married a local girl, moved to New York, and after his divorce he'd moved back to Bronco. "All I can say is Celeste is very special, Garrett."

"Have you set a date for your wedding?"

"The only thing I'm going to say is that we don't plan on having a long engagement."

Garrett nodded. "Brynn and I haven't decided on a date because she's working on revising her schedule, so she won't participate in as many rodeos as she has in the past."

Unlike Ross, Brynn Hawkins had begun curtailing her involvement in rodeo because she wanted to open a needlecraft business. She had gifted his parents with an exquisite quilt as a Thanksgiving gift and one for Jack and Audrey for their wedding.

"Has Brynn decided how many events she wants to sit out this year?"

"No," Garrett said, "but hopefully she'll make up her mind so we can set a date. My mother wants us to have the wedding at the Flying A Ranch. Plus, I'm forty-five. I'd like to become a father before I'm fifty."

Ross laughed. "You still have a couple of years before you turn the big five-oh, so I wouldn't worry too much about that."

The two men exchanged rough hugs, and Ross realized he would run into more folks in Bronco before the day ended once the news of his engagement to Celeste Montgomery spread like a lighted fuse attached to a stick of dynamite. And when the photographs of their wedding were posted on social media there was certain to be fireworks in Bronco and at the television affiliate. Celeste was not only a familiar face to millions of viewers but also a popular sports reporter. It was day two and so far, it looked like their ruse was working.

Celeste was greeted with a friendly smile from an attractive middle-aged woman as she entered the elegant bridal shop. There were racks of wedding gowns and she'd hoped to find one that would fit without undergoing extensive alterations.

"How may I help you, miss…"

"It's Celeste Montgomery. I'm looking for a gown and accessories for my upcoming wedding."

"Have you set a date?"

"Yes. It's in two days."

The woman's gray-green eyes grew wide. "That soon?"

Celeste smiled. "Yes." She leaned close enough for the other shoppers and sales personnel not to overhear what she was going to say. "We plan to elope."

"Oh, how romantic. I'm Helene and I'm certain you will find one you like in our varied selections. Are you looking for a particular style?"

Celeste had no idea of what she wanted. "What would you suggest?"

"Looking at your body I'd say a sheath. It'll show off your curves." The woman led her to the dressing room. "I'll pull a few gowns to get you started."

Celeste lost track of the number of dresses she'd tried on until she stared at herself in the full-length mirror, going completely still. A train of cascading lace entwined with silver threads on the white strapless silk sheath with a silver cummerbund appeared as if it had been made expressly for her.

Helene folded her hands in a prayerful gesture. "It's perfect. Ross Burris won't be able to take his eyes off you once he sees you in this gown."

Celeste turned to stare at Helene. "You know Ross?"

"Of course. You'd have to be living under a rock not to know the Burrises. They're local heroes here in Montana and there aren't too many places where they aren't recognized. And I'm certain everyone in Bronco will be talking about seeing Ross kissing a woman who just happened to be going into a bridal shop."

Celeste forced a saccharine smile. Ross had warned her that word would spread quickly, and she wondered if he'd ever been involved with someone from his hometown, because all the online chatter was about him and women in different cities.

"Well, as they say, the cat's out of the bag."

"I wish you and Ross the best, and I'm here to tell you that I never believed any of that mess people posted on social media about him. He and his brothers have always been honorable. I'm sure he didn't have anything to do with those women who were throwing their panties at him." She made a sucking sound with her tongue and teeth. "Some women can be so shameless whenever they meet a celebrity."

Celeste knew exactly what Helene was talking about. She'd interviewed athletes who had told her off the record that they'd encountered female fans who'd waited outside the doors of arenas for them to come out; one basketball player was forced to hire a bodyguard to thwart the advances of the more aggressive fans.

Celeste rested a hand on her hip as she examined herself in the mirror. "I think I'm going to take this one."

"You're in luck, Celeste, because you'll be able to walk out the door with the dress. Now let's look at accessories…"

Helene helped Celeste select a veil and shoes, even silk underwear.

One of the sales assistants was ringing up her purchases when Ross walked in. "Did you find everything you wanted?"

"Yes, I did. And my gown doesn't need any alterations."

"Good. I'll have to go back to The Dashing Cattleman tomorrow to pick up my tuxedo for a final fitting." Reaching into the pocket of his jeans he took out a credit card and extended it to the cashier.

The woman gave him a puzzled look. "But Miss Montgomery already gave me her credit card. I was just about to total out her purchases."

"Please give it back to her and use this one."

"Ross, I can pay—" Her protest died on her lips when he ran the back of his hand over her cheek.

"Bae, I thought we'd agreed never to argue about money."

"I'm not arguing," she said sotto voce. "It's just that I can pay for my own clothes." Adding in the purchase at the jewelry store, the amount of money Ross was spending on her would not have been troubling for Celeste if theirs was a real marriage. But she and Ross were playing a game. Albeit a game that was beginning to feel all too real to Celeste. And even though she knew how it would end, instinct told her it wasn't going to end as smoothly as they'd originally planned.

"Why are you pouting?" Ross asked Celeste when they got to the house.

She turned and glared at him. "For your information I don't pout."

"If you weren't pouting, then why haven't you said a single word during the drive back here?"

"I didn't say anything because I don't believe in airing our dirty linen in public."

A frown appeared between his eyes. "What are you talking about?"

"You embarrassed me, Ross Burris, when you exchanged my credit card for yours. Maybe the salesclerk thought my card would be declined because I didn't have enough available credit."

"I'm sorry I embarrassed you. But I'm the kind of man who'd take care of his wife, even financially."

"But when we started this little…scheme you said money shouldn't be changing hands."

"And that still stands. I paid for your ring and your wedding clothes because I wanted to. It has become a tradition for my brothers to buy rings for their fiancées from Beaumont and Rossi's." He took a step closer and cradled her face in his hands. "I know pretending we're in love isn't easy for either of us, but now that the curtain has gone up on our playacting, we must see it through until the final scene. First, we must convince the folks in Bronco that we're in love, then those who follow us online. And that can't happen if we're not on the same page."

Celeste knew Ross was right. "Next time try to give me a heads-up and preface whatever you intend to say or do with a code word."

"That sounds reasonable. Do you have nickname I can call you?"

She lowered her eyes. "My friends used to call me Cissy."

Ross dropped his hands. "Cissy is cute."

"It was cute until one boy in middle school called me pissy."

"Middle school boys are jerks."

"Were you ever a jerk?"

"I suppose I was to one girl I really liked. But I was too shy to let her know how I felt because she was one of the more popular girls in the school, so whenever we passed each other in the halls I couldn't look at her."

"Have you ever had a serious relationship with someone in Bronco?"

"No. I've dated girls who live here, but it never progressed to the serious stage."

Celeste smiled. "That's good to know because I don't want women in my face accusing me of taking their man."

Ross also smiled. "That's never going to happen, sweetheart."

It was the second time Ross had called Celeste sweetheart and she wondered if it was an endearment he called all women, or if he was rehearsing for a winning performance for his family. Celeste didn't mind pretending she was in love with Ross, but she wondered if she would be adept enough to fool the Burrises. His mother in particular, because mothers had a sixth sense when it came to ascertaining whether their children were being truthful.

"Are you going to show me your gown?" Ross asked, breaking into her thoughts.

"No! It's bad luck for the groom to see his bride in her dress before the wedding."

Ross laughed and shook his head. "Now you want to be traditional when what we have is anything but."

"I know our marriage won't be real but there are some aspects of it I'd like to be traditional."

Ross sobered and gave her a long, penetrating stare. "We may not be a traditional couple, but I don't want you forget that our marriage will become real *and* legal once we exchange vows."

Celeste nodded. It was apparent Ross had immersed himself in the role of a man in love, while she still had to remind herself to follow their carefully prepared script to pull off what she'd begun to think of as a charade she would remember long after their divorce. And what she didn't want to acknowledge was that she was beginning to have feelings for the man who was to become her husband.

Ross appeared to be everything DeAndre wasn't. He was willing to be open and honest with her. He had concocted a plan, outlined the rules, so that she would know how it would end.

Chapter Five

Celeste waited for Ross to direct the bellhop as to where to leave their luggage. Her husband-to-be had taken care of everything, not just the flight to Vegas and a luxury hotel with adjoining suites but a videographer to tape the ceremony. Celeste had signed a release, allowing the videographer to send the video of their wedding to Dean at the station and she predicted with certainty that he would air it the next day.

She shivered slightly when Ross walked over to her, and she felt a whisper of his warm breath on the nape of her neck. She wanted to tell him he was standing much too close; she could feel his body heat and smell the lingering scent of his cologne. How was she going to spend a month with a man whose very presence reminded her of how long it had been since she'd had any personal interaction with a man? It was torture being in the same room with him because whenever he looked at her, she wanted to tell him she'd made a mistake agreeing to become his wife in name only. That he was a constant reminder of what had been missing in her life for the past two years. That she'd missed being made love to, and that now she wouldn't be experiencing mental anguish if no sex hadn't been a condition of their agreement.

She sidestepped, eager to pull away from him. "Do you think it's too late for me to make an appointment with the hotel hair salon?"

Ross wrapped an arm around her waist, easing her back against his body. "I can call and find out. Perhaps I can also get a haircut and a shave."

His hard chest had her pulse racing. "Please."

It wasn't until he'd walked away that Celeste was able to draw a normal breath, and she wondered if Ross knew what he was doing to her. That each time he touched her, even in playacting, it had become harder and harder for her to remain unaffected.

Ross knew he was playing with fire whenever he touched or kissed Celeste when they were behind closed doors, where they didn't have to pretend they were in love; he was aware that he had to be careful—very, very careful not to blur the lines where their charade would become a reality. And what he was attempting to figure out was why Celeste was so different from other women he'd met and a few with whom he'd become physically involved. Back at his ranch he'd spent a sleepless night tossing in the bedroom across from hers and had only found some shuteye while watching TV in the family room.

"What do you feel like eating?" Ross asked, as he flipped through the pages in the hotel binder listing services and amenities.

"Something light. Anything big and I won't be able to fit into my gown."

"You know I'm really curious to see what you're going to wear."

Celeste smiled. "You won't have long to wait."

Ross knew she was right. Their ceremony was scheduled for seven and later that evening they'd planned to share a celebratory dinner in their suite. He and Celeste would spend Wednesday and Thursday in Vegas to give her time to write her story and send it and more photos of their wedding to Dean, before flying back to Montana Friday afternoon.

After booking appointments at the salon and ordering a

light lunch, Ross glanced at the clock on the bedside table. Once again time seemed as if it was going at warp speed, as it had since the first time he'd seen Celeste Montgomery walk into DJ's Deluxe. What he hadn't known when he'd agreed to meet her was life as he'd known it up until that time would change dramatically. Now he was going to marry her.

Celeste could not pull her eyes away from Ross when he entered her suite wearing a dark gray three-piece tuxedo, white shirt, black shoestring tie, white Stetson, and low-heeled black boots.

She smiled at him. "You look very nice, cowboy."

Ross nodded. "And you look beautiful."

Celeste's smile grew wider. He'd said she was beautiful, and she felt beautiful. When she'd left the salon, it was with professional makeup and her hair styled in an elaborate twist. "Thank you."

"There's no need to thank me, because it's true. I don't think you know just how beautiful you are."

Celeste studied Ross's face, feature by feature, unable to believe she would call this handsome, charming cowboy her husband—albeit temporarily. And she wanted to tell Ross that she felt beautiful whenever they were together.

He extended his hand. "Are you ready?"

Celeste took his hand and smiled. "Yes."

And she was. Celeste was ready to marry Ross, and she was more than ready for the next phase of her career. She knew marrying Ross Burris was certain to generate a lot of publicity on and off camera, and she intended to use it to boost her career as well as the ratings for the network.

A half hour later Celeste stood next to Ross in the Little White Wedding Chapel repeating her vows while wondering what it would be like if she and Ross truly meant the words they were speaking to each other.

Quickly she admonished herself. They might be legally married and living together, but their marriage had an expiration date. She had thirty days to share her life, and not her bed, with her new husband.

Ross dipped his head to kiss his wife but not before he caught a glimpse of tears in her eyes and wondered if they were tears of regret or joy, hoping they were the latter. He knew when he'd concocted the scheme to marry that Celeste was vulnerable. Had he taken advantage of her vulnerability to reverse the negative hits to his character? At the time he'd believed asking Celeste to marry him was a publicity stunt that would help her career, but now he wondered if his motives were more selfish than altruistic. Nevertheless, he kissed Celeste, sealing their promise to each other. This kiss was different from those they'd demonstrated in public. It was tender, intimate, and wholly satisfying and when it ended, he was rewarded with a bright smile from his wife.

Yes. Now he could call Celeste his wife.

The hired videographer had captured the entire ceremony on tape, and he would accompany them back to the hotel and continue taping until Ross closed the door to their suite, leaving what was to follow to the public's imagination.

Celeste was smiling so much that her face was beginning to ache as she walked hand in hand with Ross in the hotel lobby toward the elevators, the videographer following. Some hotel guests applauded as they watched the bride in a stunning gown with a veil and train made entirely of lace and her cowboy husband with his white Stetson. If they had wanted publicity, they got it when a woman recognized Ross and called out his name, Ross acknowledging her with a wave.

Celeste had become aware of how popular her husband was when more people recognized him. She, who hadn't known Ross Burris existed before coming to Montana, now realized she was married to a celebrity. That Ross belonged to a family that was rodeo royalty.

When they reached their floor, the videographer began filming again as Ross opened the door to their suite, swept Celeste up into his arms, and carried her inside. It was only when the door closed behind them, and the videographer left that she felt as if she could draw a normal breath.

Celeste held on to Ross's neck as he carried her into his connecting suite and placed her on his bed, his body following hers down. He removed his hat, lowered his head, and covered her mouth in a kiss that stole the breath from her lungs. The sound of her moan brought her to her senses. "Ross, we can't."

Immediately he pulled back, holding his hands palm out. "I'm sorry. I shouldn't have done that."

"It's okay, Ross. I think we both got carried away."

"No, bae, it was me who got carried away. I know we agreed there was to be no sex, but something in my brain told me it is expected for a man to make love to his wife on their wedding night."

"What you have to remember, Ross, is that our marriage is in name only. You set down the rules and I agreed to go along with them. There is a part of me that wishes that we could've met under a different set of circumstances, but that's not the case, so we, as you've said, must stick to the script before the curtain comes down on the final act."

"You're right. It won't happen again." He rolled off the bed, then helped Celeste sit up. "Are you ready to eat?"

"Yes. Let's eat in my suite. But I want to change first."

Ross nodded, watching as she walked through the connecting door, closing it behind her. He'd asked for connecting suites because he knew there was no way he could sleep in the same bed as Celeste and remain unaffected. He knew they would be able to fulfill the terms of their agreement if they did not share a bed, because for Ross that was a deal breaker. He had given his word and those who were familiar with Ross Burris knew he was a man of his word.

Celeste exchanged her veil and gown for a tank top and drawstring pants, her fancy French twist for a ponytail, and then wiped off her makeup. She was pulling on a pair of colorful ankle socks when Ross knocked, then entered her suite wearing a black T-shirt and sweatpants.

Tease. Was he aware that whenever he wore a T-shirt, she wasn't able to stop gawking at his muscular shoulders and biceps? Her husband was a perfect masculine specimen.

Ross winked at her. "I'm going to call room service to have them bring our dinner."

Fifteen minutes later she sat across the table from Ross, after he seated her, staring as he uncovered dish after dish. Celeste hadn't been able to make up her mind, so Ross seemed to have ordered some of everything.

"Will we be able to eat all of this?" she asked Ross as he poured chilled champagne into delicate flutes.

"What you don't eat I'll finish."

Celeste smiled. "What about your strict diet, Ross?"

He handed her a flute. "I'm not on a diet. What I try to do is eat healthy."

"You eat healthy and work out."

"I only work out when I'm on the circuit."

"You wouldn't have to wait to go on the circuit to work out if you build a fitness center on your property."

Ross met her eyes. "Do you work out?"

Celeste nodded. "Yes. I belong to a health club near the station. I find it helps relieve stress. My neck and shoulder muscles tighten up whenever I'm stressed."

Ross wiggled his fingers. "There's magic in these, so let me know when you need a massage."

"How much do you charge per session?" she teased.

The seconds ticked as he stared at her, Celeste wondering what he was thinking.

"I won't charge much." He smiled, turning on the charm. "Just a kiss."

"What?"

"A kiss, Celeste. Were you expecting me to ask for something more?"

"Oh no," she said quickly. "A kiss is okay." It was okay if it did not lead to something more. She had a feeling that once she made love to Ross there'd be no turning back.

"Let me make a toast." Ross extended his flute. "Don't count the days, make the days count."

Celeste touched her flute to his, smiling. "As we begin this brief journey together, I hope you get everything you want and deserve." She took a sip of the champagne, savoring the dryness on her palate.

Both she and Ross had alluded to a measure of time as if to remind the other that their relationship would be of a short duration. She set down her flute and picked up a plate. "Now, let's eat."

Celeste filled his plate, and then her own. She found herself drinking more champagne than usual because the spices in the Mongolian beef had triggered an unusual thirst. She'd drunk three glasses to Ross's four and she covered the flute with her hand when he uncorked the second bottle.

"No more, Ross, or I won't be able to stand up."

He refilled his flute. "You don't have to stand up. I'll carry you to bed."

Celeste refused to think about a bed and Ross at the same time because she didn't want a repeat of their earlier encounter.

"That's okay. If I drink any more, I'll end up pissy-eyed drunk. And besides, I'm as full as a tick."

Ross laughed softly. "It's been a long time since I've heard that expression."

"Well, it's true. Full and sleepy."

"Go to bed, sweetheart. I'll call room service and have them pick up everything."

"Are you sure you don't want me to help you?" she asked Ross.

"Very sure. Now, go get some rest. Sleep in as late as you want. Once you're up we'll go down and hang out at the pool."

"I didn't bring a bathing suit."

"Neither did I, but we can buy them from one of the shops."

Pushing back her chair, she stood. "I'll see you tomorrow. Good night."

Ross also stood. "Good night."

She left the dining area and entered her bedroom, closing the door behind her. She managed to brush her teeth before she pulled a nightgown over her head and got into her marriage bed.

Alone.

Ross adjusted the pillows under his head in an attempt to find a comfortable position. There was no doubt he was going to have another restless night. A night in which he should've shared the bed of the woman in the adjoining suite. A woman who was his wife.

Wife.

He groaned and ran a hand over his face. *Fool.* He had to be the king of fools to marry a woman he was forbidden to make love to. And if he'd been able to turn back the clock and renegotiate the terms of their deal, the topic of sex would not have become a condition.

He shifted and then took his frustration out on the pillows as if they'd done something to him. Ross continued to toss and turn until he decided to get out of bed and step onto the balcony. Folding his body down on a cushioned chaise, he inhaled a lungful of dry, hot desert air. Hundreds of thousands of lights lit up the strip as if it were noon rather than midnight. And if he had been a gambler he would've put on his clothes and visited one of the casinos. However, he hadn't competed as a bronc rider, each time risking injury, to throw away his winnings on the turn of a card or the spin of a wheel. There were times when he'd spent three-quarters of the year on the rodeo circuit, competing to earn enough money to pay his tuition, buy property, and invest in his after-school program. After a while, Ross had found himself dozing off and knew he should go inside but loathed moving. He lay motionless, until his breathing deepened, and he was finally embraced by Morpheus.

Streaks of color painted the desert sky when Celeste woke, moaning as she attempted to swallow but discovered her mouth was too dry. She had no one to blame but herself for drinking more champagne than she normally would. She went into the bathroom and brushed her teeth, then rinsed her mouth with a peppermint mouthwash.

Celeste opened a bottle of water and went out onto the balcony to watch the sunrise. She'd just put the bottle to her mouth when she saw Ross, wearing only a pair of pajama pants, sprawled out on a chaise, asleep, and she wondered if he'd spent the night there. She didn't know why, but Celeste felt like a voyeur watching the rise and fall of his smooth, muscled chest in slow and measured breathing.

She thought it ironic that her husband had spent their wedding night sleeping on the balcony while his new wife slept alone in a king-size bed in an adjoining suite. Even when she'd fantasized being married this wasn't the scenario Celeste could have envisioned.

The difference with this marriage, though, was it had an expiration date. Which, she reasoned, was a good thing. There wouldn't be enough time for her to develop deep feelings for her husband, so when it came time for her to leave it wouldn't be with the messy angst many couples experienced when they broke up.

She drank slowly while debating whether to return inside or sit on a matching chaise to wait for Ross to wake up. Celeste didn't have to make up her mind when Ross opened his eyes and stared at her as if she were a stranger. But she was a stranger to him and he to her. They hadn't known each other a week and they'd had one of the shortest engagement periods possible, yet they'd managed to pull off a wedding without the assistance of a wedding planner or the knowledge of their families. Families. She did not want to imagine the hoopla and blowback from the Burrises and Montgomerys once the news came out. And no doubt that would be very soon because the photos of their wedding were probably in Dean's inbox.

After taking a step, Celeste sat on a matching chaise. "Good morning, Ross. Did you sleep well?" She'd asked the question, unaware that it had come out sounding facetious.

For Ross, it wasn't so much seeing Celeste standing there when he woke, but it was what she was wearing. The full-length lacy white nightgown with thin straps and a plunging neckline revealed more of her body than it concealed. In that moment his libido went into overdrive. Karma had come, playing him back in spades, he realized. There'd been women he'd dated, slept with, and had no intention of marrying, but now that he'd married Celeste, he could not have sex with her.

Despite his love 'em and leave 'em reputation with women, Ross hadn't had that many encounters that he couldn't remember their faces or names, yet the public's perception of him wasn't kind when it came to his exploits outside of the rodeo. Ross could not understand that since he tended to be low-key when he wasn't competing and had spent most of his time studying.

Geoff's popularity in and out of rodeo had carried over to his brothers and whenever Ross told everyone who he was, he'd found himself surrounded. Especially by the female groupies. There were a few who had begun following the circuit when the Burrises were on the program and would use the most inventive detective work to uncover which hotel they were staying at and their favorite restaurant in the host cities. Ross was always polite when approached, but he drew the line at sleeping with them. His interaction with them was occasionally dinner with drinks. It had taken him a while to process the idea that when his dinner dates wanted to take a picture of them with their phones it was to post it on social media.

That was before he'd invited Celeste Montgomery to meet him for lunch at DJ's Deluxe. It was even before, when he'd overheard her conversation with her boss, that the wheels in his head had begun turning to figure out how he could help Celeste with her dilemma and get out of his. What Ross hadn't known when he presented Celeste with the plan to save her career and salvage what was left of his less than favorable reputation was that it would backfire. He should have, because from the moment Rylee handed him the press kit and he'd taken one look at Celeste's photograph he knew there was something special about her.

Meeting her in person and talking with Celeste was a new experience for Ross, because she was the first woman who'd truly listened to what he had to say. He didn't know if it was because she was a journalist or if it was her personality, but in the few days they'd spent together in Bronco Celeste had asked questions, not about him, but about the horses, his goals, his home, even his book collection.

She had begun interviewing him, asking questions that had allowed him to open up to her as he never had to any woman. And he liked it.

"Good morning, Celeste," he said after a prolonged silence.

"Did you sleep here all night?"

Ross turned to face her. "Not all night."

"Is there something wrong with your bed?"

Hell yeah. It was empty.

"No," he lied smoothly. "I was restless, and I decided to take in a little desert air and fell asleep. How did you sleep?"

Celeste smiled. "Like a baby. I only got up because I was dehydrated after drinking champagne."

Ross rested his head on his arm. "Does champagne always affect you like that?"

Celeste shifted to face him. "Yes. That's why I limit myself to two glasses."

"You like wine." The query came out like a statement.

She nodded. "I prefer wine to liquor. I don't have the tolerance for the hard stuff."

"What about beer?"

"I limit myself to one glass."

"Why do I get the impression that you place quite a few restrictions on yourself? Are you always so controlled?"

Celeste's expression changed and she frowned at him. "You call them restrictions when I look at them as limitations, because I've learned from experience when to stop or when it's best to give it up completely. Whether in relationships or situations, I know when to retreat to save myself."

Ross was surprised to hear Celeste talk about herself, because so far it had all been about him. "Save yourself from what, Celeste?"

"Danger, disappointment, and eventual heartache."

Now Ross was intrigued by the woman he'd married because he suspected she was ready to reveal details about the very private Celeste. She knew everything about him, when he hardly knew more than the names and careers of her family members.

"How many times has your heart been broken?"

A sad smile flittered over Celeste's delicate features. "Only once."

"Was that once enough for you to decide not again?"

"You could say that. However, it's different with us because we know when what we have is going to end."

A beat passed before Ross asked, "Is that what you want, Celeste? For this to be over at the end of the month?"

She nodded. "It's what I need, Ross. I've learned to live my life without second-guessing my decisions. I don't want to look back and say I should've done something differently to achieve a better outcome. If this marriage advances my career and if the positive stories I file about you dispel the negative comments so you can open the after-school center, then I know without a doubt that becoming Mrs. Ross Burris was one of, if not the best, decisions I will ever make in my life."

Ross took her hand in his. "Well, Mrs. Burris, I don't know about you, but we only have one more day in Vegas so I think we should make the best of it. I'd like us to take in some of the sights and maybe a concert while we're here. After all, we are on our honeymoon."

Smiling, Celeste said, "Mr. Burris, I like the sound of that."

Chapter Six

Celeste's cell phone dinged a programmed ringtone as she and Ross were leaving their suite. She looked at Ross. "That's Dean."

He met her eyes. "Aren't you going to answer it?" he asked, when the phone continued ringing.

She nodded, activating the speaker feature because she wanted Ross to hear her conversation with her boss. "Good afternoon, Dean."

"That it is! I just saw the footage of your wedding to Ross Burris. I must give it to you, Celeste—I had no idea you were involved with him."

She shared a smile with Ross. "That's because I wanted to keep my private life private."

"And you did just that. I suppose I should congratulate myself for sending you to Montana to interview Geoff Burris, because it gave you the perfect opportunity to hook up with your boyfriend. And that's what you meant when you said you were working on something big, and it had to do with a Burris brother."

Celeste shook her head when Dean said, "hook up." "Ross and I did not hook up, Dean. We'd decided to keep our relationship secret until we felt it was time to go public with our wedding."

"I'm glad you did," Dean continued, "because our ratings are going to go through the roof once we air this tonight. And

I'm certain our viewing audience will want to know everything about your romance with one of rodeo's superstars. I need to know how you and Burris met, and why you decided not to go public with your relationship until now. I'm going to have our arts and entertainment correspondent contact you as soon as I hang up so she can interview you."

She smiled when Ross gave her a thumbs-up motion. "When do you want to conduct the interview? I'm asking because Ross and I have plans to return to Montana tomorrow."

"I need her to interview you before you leave Vegas. And make sure Burris will be around too."

"I'll make certain of that. Is there anything else, Dean?"

"Yes. Congratulations!"

"Thank you. Text me once you schedule a time for the interview so we can be in our suite."

"Will do. Now I want you to enjoy your honeymoon."

"Thank you, Dean." Celeste ended the call, smiling. "If we're able to fool Dean, then I believe we can really pull this off," she said to Ross. "Even though my boss is what I call a blowhard he's also an incredibly perceptive journalist. It's as if he has a sixth sense when ferreting out what is factual and what is unadulterated fiction. He's fired several reporters who fabricated stories because they were on deadline."

Ross took a step and wrapped an arm around Celeste's waist. "That's why when I suggested we marry it had to be legal."

Celeste nodded. "I need to ask you something."

"What?"

"Are you ready?"

Ross's expression stilled, becoming serious. "Ready for what?"

"For the fallout when we break up after being married for such a short time. How will it look for you if you're not able to make a go of your marriage? Even if you claim you're heartbroken because you didn't want your marriage to end, some folks may blame you because of your past reputation."

"We already talked about this, Celeste. You file for divorce. I'll appear emotionally upset and tell everyone I let you go so you can advance your career, because that's something you wouldn't be able to do living in Bronco."

"Okay," she said, nodding. "I just don't want for our breakup to backfire on you."

"What if you wait a couple of months before you file for an annulment?"

"Okay," Celeste repeated.

"Thanks, Celeste," he said, a smile flirting with his mouth. "I do believe you care."

Oh, she cared about him, all right. A lot more than she'd wanted to admit.

Ross released her waist and cradled her face. "I don't want you to worry about me. When I came up with the scenario, I knew how it would end, and I'm prepared for that. What I don't want is for you to look like a victim or become a casualty. I've been in the public eye since I began competing at sixteen, so I've had ten years to deal with the highs and the lows when it comes to my career and reputation."

Celeste held on to his wrists. "But I do worry about you because you're my husband."

Ross schooled his expression not to react to her touching entreaty. Celeste was worried about him; she cared for him. If he wasn't careful, he would find himself in too deep where he would do everything in his power to stop Celeste from leaving Bronco.

Lowering his head, he brushed a light kiss over her soft parted lips. "Thank you for your concern, bae, but I'll be all right." What Ross had to do was convince himself that he would be all right after losing Celeste.

"If you say so," she whispered against his mouth.

"It is so," he countered. "Now, didn't you say you wanted to do some shopping before we leave for Bronco?"

"I want to stop in a souvenir shop to buy a Las Vegas T-shirt. I try to buy a T-shirt from every city I visit, and Vegas is one I need to add to my collection."

"Let's go, then. We'll need to get back for the interview. It's going to be fun to watch my wife do her thing."

Celeste grinned. "Just hope your wife will be able to pull it off where folks will believe me when I say the first time I met this rodeo cowboy I knew he was the one with whom I wanted to spend the rest of my life."

"That's right, because it was the same with me," Ross said. The only difference was he was beginning to think that was no lie.

After a successful trip to a souvenir shop and an all-you-can-eat elaborate buffet, they were on the way back to the hotel.

They were only feet from their hotel when a young woman wearing a cowboy hat, boots, and Daisy Dukes smiled at Ross and said, "Aren't you Ross Burris?" He nodded, and her smile became a full grin where Celeste was able to see almost all the way to her molars. "I thought so. I saw you win top prize in the bronc riding competition in Oklahoma a couple of years ago." Reaching for her tote she took out a marker and handed it to Ross. "Would you mind autographing my arm?"

Celeste was shocked that he would comply and write on the woman's arm and wondered where else he had put his name on other women's bodies. Even before she could react a small crowd had gathered asking for Ross's autograph. He graciously scrawled his name on whatever was extended to him, and Celeste stared at his profile under the shadow of his Stetson as he smiled and said words of encouragement to young boys who said they wanted to join the rodeo. At that moment she knew her husband was a hero to a lot of people despite the negative comments written about him on social media.

"Mrs. Burris, my name is Philip Robbins. Would you mind posing with your husband so I can take a picture of you both?"

She turned to find a man holding a camera used by professional photographers, and wondered if he was paparazzi. Perfect, she thought.

"Yes, but you have to wait for him to finish signing autographs for his fans."

"I was able to photograph you last night when you had just come back from your wedding and it came out beautifully, but I'd like another shot with you wearing street clothes before I add it to my collection," the photographer admitted.

Celeste moved closer to him. "Can you show me what you took last night?"

Her jaw dropped slightly when he showed her the photos he'd taken in the lobby of the hotel once they'd returned from the wedding chapel. There was one where she and Ross were facing each other, and she was smiling at him. And another when Ross had dipped his head to kiss her cheek. Philip Robbins had managed to get off a third shot with them holding hands while waiting for the elevator. If pictures could speak, then they would say these were two people in love.

"Do you like them, Mrs. Burris?"

She smiled at the slightly built elderly bearded man. "Very much. Are you a professional photographer?"

"I was before I retired. Now I volunteer teaching young kids who are interested in photography. I believe most of them are more impressed with who I have photographed than learning about lighting and camera angles."

Celeste listened intently when he mentioned the names of sports figures, politicians, singers, dancers, and foreign officials and dignitaries before Ross signed his last autograph. She told him what Mr. Robbins wanted. Ross appeared to be as impressed and pleased with what the man had shot when he showed him the prior night's photos.

"Let's make this good," he whispered in her ear as he pulled her close to his side. "Is it all right if I kiss you?"

"Yes," she whispered as a flush warmed her face. Other than the kiss they'd exchanged to seal their marriage, and the few chaste ones in Bronco, they hadn't been effusive in exhibiting PDAs.

Again, a small crowd had gathered to watch Celeste and Ross pose for pictures. Whistles and applause followed when Ross swept Celeste up in his arms and kissed her. She felt heat everywhere when he deepened the kiss and she clung to his neck as if he were her lifeline. She realized when Ross ended the kiss and set her on her feet that Mr. Robbins wasn't the only one taking pictures. She was sure the onlookers' photos would appear on the internet.

"We couldn't afford to pay for that type of publicity," Ross said, once they were back in her suite.

Celeste flopped down on the love seat and kicked off her running shoes. "There's nothing better than free publicity, and it looks like we've gotten an overabundance of it with you autographing your fans."

Ross sat down next to her. "Don't forget our kissing scene."

Shifting slightly, she rested her bare feet over his thigh. "*Your* kissing scene, Ross."

He gave her toes a gentle squeeze. "Well, I had to make it look good."

"And you did," she said. "Once folks see those pictures, they will believe the bad boy has truly been redeemed."

Resting his head against the back cushion, Ross smiled. "And all because I met a beautiful reporter who took my breath away the first time I met her."

"Don't you think you're coming on a little too strong?"

Ross chuckled. "That's only the beginning, sweetheart.

I have a few other lines in my repertoire that are certain to make you blush."

She sat up. "No thanks, Ross. I don't need to hear them."

He sobered and gave her a direct stare. "What's the matter, Celeste?"

"We'd agreed that what we have is an act, so I don't want you to go off script. And I certainly don't need you and your lines messing with my head. We're leaving here tomorrow and I'm willing to bet that your parents are going to want to know what's going on, and if I don't have my thoughts straight then they're going to know we're living a lie."

He took her hand and squeezed it. "Okay, I'll cool it and we'll stick to the script."

Celeste didn't know why she was beginning to feel like Ross was blaming her for erecting barriers because something nagged at her that he wanted more from his wife than she was willing to give.

Celeste activated the camera on her laptop and then adjusted the volume before she began her Zoom meeting with the station's arts and entertainment correspondent. After she and Ross had returned to the suite, she'd received a text message for the interview to go live at two Pacific time. That gave her enough time to curl her hair, apply makeup, and change into a black sheath dress along with her requisite pearls. Ross had also changed into a snap button white shirt, jeans, boots, and his ubiquitous Stetson.

Nikki Harper's image appeared on the screen. "I must say before we begin the interview that marriage agrees with you, Celeste."

Celeste smiled. "Thank you, Nikki."

"I can't wait to see the man who has you grinning like a Cheshire cat."

"You will." The plan was for Celeste to be interviewed alone first, then Nikki would bring in Ross.

"We've got thirty seconds to air," Nikki said, "then I'm going to share the screen so the viewers can see both of us."

Celeste smiled when Ross, sitting out of camera range, gave her a thumbs-up. She affected what she called her professional face once the session began.

"This is Nikki Harper reporting to you from WWCH-TV in Chicago, and today I'm honored to interview one of our own. You know her as Celeste Montgomery, but as of yesterday Celeste married popular bronc rider Ross Burris in Las Vegas. Celeste, how was it you and Ross were able to keep your relationship so secret?"

"It was easy because both of us have schedules that take us to different cities at different times."

"Are you saying he was able to slip in and out of Chicago without anyone recognizing him?"

Celeste laughed softly. "Yes. But you'll have to ask him how he managed to do that."

Nikki also laughed. "You can be certain I will. Now, Celeste, tell me how you two met."

Straight-faced, Celeste repeated the rehearsed scenario she and Ross had crafted about meeting in Fort Worth and how it had been love at first sight. "I'm ashamed to say that as a sports correspondent I didn't know who he was because I never followed the rodeo, and cowboys aren't a big deal in Chicago."

"I'm certain there's going to be more interest now that you're married to a rodeo superstar." Nikki paused. "I must admit that when I went online to look up Ross Burris's name, I was shocked by some of the negative comments posted about him. Did or does that bother you?"

"No, because what has been written is the furthest from the truth. My husband is gracious to his fans, but sometimes people want more than he can give, and they post nasty comments. My husband has managed to earn an undergraduate and a graduate degree in education in addition to his rodeo accolades."

"That's quite an accomplishment."

Celeste smiled and lowered her eyes. "I agree."

"Does he plan to teach?"

She raised her head to look directly at the camera. "His future plan includes opening a no-fee after-school enrichment center where students in Bronco could come for help with their homework or test prep."

"That's really commendable."

"Both his parents are educators. His mother is a kindergarten teacher, and his father is a high school principal."

"It looks as if he has wonderful role models."

"That he does," Celeste said, smiling.

"Now, back to you Celeste. You say you and Ross met in January of this year and what made you decide to elope?"

"Ross and I hadn't planned to elope, but when I got an assignment to go to Bronco, Montana, to interview his brother Geoff Burris it was like the stars were all aligned because it was the first time I got to see Ross on his own turf. Geoff wasn't available because he and his fiancée are on an extended vacation in Europe, so that's when Ross decided that we should go public with our relationship."

"By going public he meant getting married?"

"Yes."

"How much time elapsed from when you decided to elope?"

"Three days."

Nikki laughed as she shook her head. "You didn't waste any time. I saw the videos of your wedding and I can't believe you pulled it together in three days."

Celeste also laughed. "I surprised myself." She mentioned Ever After and The Dashing Cattleman, deciding to give the Bronco businesses some free advertising.

"You did all of this in Bronco?"

"Yes. Ross wanted a Western-style tuxedo."

"Just seeing the video I'd say your husband is every inch the quintessential cowboy." Nikki paused as she glanced down at her notes. "Would your husband mind if I ask him a few questions I'm certain our viewers would like the answers to?"

"Not at all."

She waited until Ross came over to sit next to her and took her hand. Celeste was certain the proprietary gesture wasn't lost on Nikki. She successfully hid a smile when she noticed Nikki's reaction to seeing Ross up close. Her mouth opened slightly as if she was forced to take a breath. Celeste knew what Nikki was thinking and feeling because she'd reacted the same way the first time she came face-to-face with Ross Burris.

Nikki recovered quickly. "Firstly, I'd like to congratulate you on your marriage to my colleague, and secondly, I wish you all the best when you set up your after-school enrichment program."

"Thank you," Ross said with a barely perceptible nod.

Nikki cleared her throat. "Now, Ross. What is there about Celeste that made you want to marry her?"

"There aren't enough hours in the day for me to list all of the things I truly love about this woman."

"Oh." The single word was pregnant with emotion as Nikki glanced down at her notes. "I supposed you answered that question for me." She paused, then said, "What has been your reaction to all the things posted online about you? Does it upset you?"

"I wasn't upset because personally I know none of them are true. It only matters that my family knows I'm not the villain the world makes me out to be."

"Speaking of your character..."

"What about it?" Ross asked. His voice was shaded in a neutral tone.

"Being photographed with a lot of women doesn't bother you?"

"No, I can't control what people do or say. I've lost track of the number of times women have asked me to take a picture with them, but for me it's nothing personal. I've had one serious relationship but that was in the past. But once I met Celeste, I knew she was special and different from any other woman I'd met or known. So special that I found myself in love with her almost immediately. Four months later I knew for certain that I wanted to marry her."

"Whose idea was it to keep your relationship a secret?"

Celeste and Ross shared a look. "Both of us," they said in unison.

"Why the secrecy, Ross?"

He gave Nikki what Celeste interpreted as a death stare. "Because I didn't want her life upended once people discovered we were dating. She didn't need the paparazzi shadowing her every move whenever she was on assignment."

"But won't that happen now that she's married to you?"

"I don't believe so. Reporters are always looking for a scoop, but now that we're married there's nothing left to uncover." He raised Celeste's left hand and kissed the back of it.

"I know you live in Montana, while Celeste works in Chicago. Will this prove problematic because you'll have a long-distance marriage?"

"Not at all. Celeste and I will manage our schedules. And when we're off at the same time we'll spend it together in Montana."

Nikki nodded. "I think I've run out of time. Again, I congratulate you on your marriage and wish you both the best for your future. This is Nikki Harper reporting from WWCH-TV. Thank you for watching."

Nikki's screen went dark, and Celeste and Ross looked at each other, then burst out laughing.

"What do you think?" Celeste asked.

"I think it went quite well. Nikki wasn't reticent when she questioned me about my experience with other women. She asked and I told her the truth."

"I'm glad you did, Ross. Nikki said the interview will air tonight along with the videos of our wedding."

"Good," Ross said. "You know you made me look better than I am."

"No, I didn't because everything I said about you is the truth."

He smiled. "So, you're beginning to like this rogue cowboy?"

Her smile matched his. "I'm past beginning, Ross. I do like you."

Ross stared down at her under lowered lids. Reaching up he removed his hat as if in slow motion and set it on a side table as his head dipped, and he kissed Celeste for the second time that day. But this kiss was different from the others they'd shared. His tongue sent shivers of desire through her body that quickly spiraled out of control. Her mouth was on fire. Her body was on fire. And she wanted Ross to quench the flames.

Ross cupped her hips and lifted Celeste off her feet to feel the hardness in his groin he was helpless to control. He wanted Celeste. In his bed.

Her arms tightened around his neck as he deepened the kiss, his tongue dueling with hers for dominance. Without warning, realization hit Ross and he knew if he didn't stop then he wouldn't be able to stop. He didn't want to become the "dog," women had labeled him when they claimed he took advantage of them. Celeste wasn't just another woman. She was his wife and he'd promised her he would honor their agreement, because that was what she wanted.

He ended the kiss, set Celeste on her feet, and buried his face against her velvety soft neck. Ross knew he would never tire of kissing her mouth and inhaling her perfume. Ross knew he had to get out of the suite before he sabotaged whatever plans he'd made to see their pretense to its conclusion. Thankfully they were returning to Bronco the next day where he would have the ranch to distract him from focusing solely on Celeste.

"I'm going downstairs to check out some of the shops to see if I can find something for the guy who takes care of the horses. Do you want me to bring you anything?"

Celeste shook her head. "No. I'm good here."

Ross turned on his heel. She was good while he felt as if he didn't know whether he was coming or going. They were married, would live together, and pretend that they were madly in love while knowing it would come crashing down around them at the end of the month.

If Celeste was counting down the days when she would return to Chicago, then Ross had begun counting the days praying he would survive the greatest challenge when it came to letting Celeste go.

Chapter Seven

Ross checked his phone within minutes of the plane touching down and saw that he had four text messages—all from his mother. He read the latest one first:

Please come see me as soon as you get back.

Are you okay?

Have you lost your mind?

What in the world have you done?

There was no doubt Jeanne Burris had seen the interview and the video of his wedding and thought perhaps he had taken leave of his senses. She knew nothing about him dating anyone. And if he was serious about a woman, then surely, he would've introduced her to his family.

He waited until he retrieved his pickup from the airport parking lot to tell Celeste he was taking her to meet his parents.

"Now?"

"Yes now. My mother has been blowing up my phone with text messages asking if I've lost my mind."

Celeste gave him a sidelong glance. "She's not the only one who believes we've lost our minds. My mother hasn't contacted me because she probably hasn't seen the video. But when she does, Sandra Montgomery is going to turn into the Incredible Hulk."

"What about your father?"

"Dad is chill."

"So, I don't have to concern myself that he's going to come looking for me with a shotgun."

"That's not funny, Ross." She closed her eyes. "I don't know if I'm ready to meet your parents."

He rested his right hand on her thigh as he steered with his left. "You were spectacular during the interview, so you shouldn't have a problem convincing my family that we love each other."

Celeste had embellished facts for her interview with Nikki Harper, but that was different from lying outright to Ross's parents. And as Celeste Burris, she was now a daughter-in-law and a sister-in-law, and she was about to lie to people who were expected to welcome her into their family.

"Can't we stop at home so I can change into something more appropriate?" she asked Ross.

"You look beautiful."

Celeste rolled her eyes at him. Ballet flats, leggings, and a smock-like shirt weren't what she thought of as appropriate for meeting her in-laws for the first time. She turned her head and stared out the side window.

She knew when she agreed to marry Ross that she would eventually have to meet his family. Her concern was whether they would blame her for forcing Ross into marriage when he'd appeared to have lived his life by his leave.

All too soon the drive ended as Ross maneuvered into a driveway and parked. The front door opened, and Celeste experienced a momentary panic that gnawed at the fragile shred of confidence she'd hung on to when she saw Ross's mother in the doorway. She waited for Ross to get out and come around to open the door for her.

"Just remember we love each other," he whispered, as he helped her out of the pickup.

Celeste nodded, smiling. "Okay."

Her smile was still in place as she approached Ross's mother. She saw Jeanne take a surreptitious glance at her hand with the diamond band. Celeste wasn't certain how to address the older woman and waited for Ross to make the introductions.

Ross dipped his head and kissed Jeanne's cheek. "Hi, Mom."

"Hello, Ross. So, the rumors are true. You're married."

Ross rested a hand at the small of Celeste's back. "Yes. Celeste and I were married in Vegas a couple of days ago."

Jeanne gave Celeste a long, penetrating stare before smiling. She then extended both hands to Celeste. "Welcome to the family."

Celeste was certain Jeanne heard her exhale a breath of relief. "Thank you so much, Mrs. Burris."

"Jeanne will do, because right now there are quite a few Mrs. Burrises."

"Would you mind if I call you Miss Jeanne?" It was the way she'd been raised.

"Of course not, dear. Please come sit with me and tell me why I had to learn my son felt the need to fly off to Vegas to marry rather than do it here in Bronco."

"We were going to tell you once we got back," Ross said.

"We would've liked to have known before you eloped," Benjamin Burris said, walking into the living room. He gave Celeste a gentle hug before he sat on the sofa next to his wife. "Is there a reason why you *had* to marry so quickly?"

"No, Dad. Celeste and I may have been impulsive once we eloped, but what we feel for each other is real. We're in love, and we decided we didn't want to wait." Celeste moved closer to Ross on the love seat, smiling when he reached for her hand.

"Do you love my son?" Jeanne asked Celeste.

"Yes," she said quickly. "I love him very much."

"How long have you two been dating?"

Jeanne's question was not lost on Celeste. She knew Ross's mother was testing her. If she'd seen the video as she said, she'd know the answer.

"Since January."

"That's not very long to get to know each other," Jeanne countered.

"Mom, Celeste, and I have the rest of our lives to get to know each other. I'm certain you and Dad are still learning things about each other after nearly forty years."

"True," Benjamin confirmed. "But your mother and I were shocked when folks were talking about seeing you with a woman in Beaumont and Rossi's Fine Jewels looking at rings. And when they asked me about it, I was forced to say no comment."

"I'm sorry about that, Dad."

"How about your folks, Celeste?" Jeanne questioned. "Do they know you're married?"

"Not yet. I'd planned to call them today with the news."

Jeanne smiled. "Well, now that the two of you are back, I want you to come over later for dinner. Jack and Audrey and Mike and Corinne will be joining us."

Ross dropped an arm over Celeste's shoulders. "You'll get to meet everyone except Geoff and Stephanie."

Celeste wanted to leave because she wanted to call her parents with the news she was married, that is if they hadn't already watched the televised interview.

Jeanne clasped her hands. "I know you've been traveling and need to unwind before tonight, so can we count on seeing you tonight?"

Ross stood up, reaching back to help Celeste to her feet. "Yes. We'll see you later."

Benjamin walked over and hugged Celeste again. "Now we have four sons and four daughters."

Going on tiptoe, Celeste kissed his cheek. "Thank you."

"No, thank you, for marrying my son, because now I hope folks can stop all that ugly talk about him and other women."

"I hope it stops too," she said to Benjamin. Not only was it half the reason for this sham marriage, but she also wanted it stopped for Ross's sake. Because she cared for him.

Too much.

"It feels good to be home," Ross said, as he unlocked the front door to his house. He turned back to Celeste, swooped her up in his arms, and shouldered the door open. "It's tradition for a man to carry his wife over the threshold for the first time."

Celeste held on to his neck. "But this is the second time you've done this."

"I know, but this is the one that counts."

"Do you think your folks believed our story, Ross?"

He set her on her feet. "I hope they did. What do you think?"

"I think your mother is more suspicious than your father. Mothers know when their children are lying, Ross."

"Well, you didn't lie when you said that we're recognizable. Remember when we were in the jewelry store and Tiffany said that she recognized you from a YouTube video. There are millions of Tiffanys out there who have watched you. It's the same with me with folks who follow rodeo."

"That was obvious when you were signing autographs in Vegas."

"That's because one of the rodeo circuits is in Nevada. It's called the Wilderness Circuit, located east of California, and includes Nevada, Utah, and the majority of Idaho. The Montana Circuit includes the entire state of Montana, and the Mountain States Circuit takes in Wyoming and Colorado."

"I had no idea rodeo was so popular."

"Not only is it popular," Ross confirmed, "but there's a lot of money to be made in the sport. But we'll talk about that at another time. I know you want to call your folks."

"Thank you, Ross."

She climbed the staircase to the second floor and walked into the bedroom she knew, despite being married, she would not share with her husband. Taking out her phone, she tapped the contact for her parents' home number. It rang three times before she heard her father's greeting.

"Hi, Dad. How are you?"

"That's what I should be asking you, Celeste. Your mother wanted to call you when she saw you on television last night, but I told her to wait because you would call and straighten out everything. She has an appointment so she's not home."

Celeste sat on a cushioned bench at the foot of the king-size bed, grateful her mother wasn't home. "There's nothing to straighten out, Dad."

She told Thomas Montgomery the same story she'd told Nikki Harper, and Jeanne and Benjamin Burris. She'd repeated the lie so often that Celeste was beginning to believe it herself. Her explanation seemed to satisfy her father, who said he would tell her mother why she'd opted to elope rather than have a traditional wedding. She ended the call, grateful that it had been her father and not her mother who'd answered the phone, so she wouldn't have to deal with Sandra's histrionics. Now, she had to face Ross's brothers and sisters-in-law. And if she could convince them that she and Ross had married for love, then she would think of herself as home free.

Ross unloaded their luggage from the truck, left Celeste's outside her bedroom, and then returned to the pickup to drive over to check on his horses. He'd trusted Jeremy Shepherd to see after the small herd whenever he was away because he was part of the deal when Ross purchased the property. The former owners had hired Jeremy to care for the horses when he returned to Bronco after several deployments. Jeremy had avoided physical injury but had not escaped psychological trauma and had been diagnosed with PTSD. He'd moved in with his sister and her family after his wife left him because she claimed she hadn't signed up to care for a crazy person. The military veteran loved horses and Ross was beginning to think of him as a horse whisperer.

He saw Jeremy sitting on the top railing of the enclosure watching the colts. Ross got out of the truck and walked over to the fence.

"I heard you got married," Jeremy said, deadpan.

He smiled up at the bearded thirty-something man who met his eyes for several seconds. "That I did."

"Why hadn't you brought her around before?"

"I couldn't because she lived in Chicago."

"So, now she's going to live here in Bronco." Jeremy's question came out as a statement.

"Yes."

But it's only temporary. Ross couldn't tell Jeremy or anyone, and that included his family, that the status of his marriage to Celeste would be one of short duration, lasting only a month.

Now that they were back in Bronco, he would be the one to begin counting the days when Celeste would pack her bags and return to Chicago. He didn't know how it had happened, but it hadn't taken a week for Ross to get so used to being with her. It was as if six days had become six years. The few days they'd spent together in Bronco before leaving for Vegas had given him a glimpse of what his life would be like if there were no deal. If he and Celeste had met like the story they'd concocted and had had a secret liaison before deciding to marry—this time for real.

Even though they'd slept in separate bedrooms, he was able to feel her presence everywhere in the house. He got up early to groom the horses and muck out the stalls and when he returned to the house Celeste would be in the kitchen to hand him a cup of coffee. Then, after he'd showered, she'd join him for breakfast. It had become his favorite time of day.

He'd discovered her to be pleasant and upbeat, and she was the first woman who had become what he'd thought of as a companion. Someone he liked being with and someone he could talk to and know that she was listening to him. Maybe it was because of her own career as a television journalist that she wasn't starstruck around him, and therefore hadn't felt the need to flirt or attempt to seduce him.

"I heard she's beautiful," Jeremy said, breaking into Ross's thoughts.

"That she is, Jeremy."

"When am I going to meet her?"

"I'll have her come with me to your sister's place in a few days."

"I have to go see a doctor at the VA hospital in a few days because my headaches are back. He wants to run some more tests. I plan to call one of my buddies and ask him to drive me to Billings, because my sister can't get off work."

"Don't call anyone. I'll take you."

Jeremy shook his head. "You don't have to do that, Ross."

"But I want to. I'll take you there and when you call to tell me you're finished, I'll come and bring you back." Ross wanted to tell him it was the least he could do for the veteran who'd put his life on the line to serve his country.

"You know I really appreciate that."

Ross climbed up on the fence to sit several feet away from Jeremy. "And I really appreciate you taking good care of the horses."

"That's what you pay me to do."

"It has nothing to do with money, Jeremy. I don't know what it is, but the horses sense something about you that's special." The words were barely off his tongue when the colts trotted over to the fence and nudged Jeremy's legs.

"It's just that I love horses and they seem to love me back."

Ross chuckled. "I love horses, too, but not when I'm sitting on one that's intent on bucking so hard that I won't be able to stay on his back for the requisite eight seconds."

"I've watched you ride some mean-ass broncs and you've managed to stay on and win a shitload of prize money."

Jeremy was right about him ranking high enough in the sport to earn enough money for him to live comfortably. He wasn't wealthy, but at twenty-six he was astute enough to have secured financial stability.

He looked around the property. "Where's Scamp?"

"Probably at your house."

"Why my house?" Ross asked Jeremy.

"He's been sleeping on your porch at night instead of with the horses."

Ross smothered a groan. "That's probably because he's looking for my wife."

"Why her, Ross?"

"She gave him a bath before we left for Vegas."

"He let her touch him?"

"Yup."

Jeremy grunted. "There must be something special about her because he's the most panicky dog I've ever seen. He won't even let me get close to him."

Ross wanted to tell Jeremy that the woman he'd married was beyond special. He could not believe how confident she'd looked when they'd watched the taped interview together the night before. And it hadn't mattered that she'd appeared in front of the camera countless times, he'd found himself mes-merized by her image and how natural she was when recounting their scripted story. And each time they were forced to reveal how they'd met and why they'd elected to keep their relationship secret, Ross wanted the lies to be true.

"I brought a little something back for you from Vegas. I'll drop it off at your place sometime tomorrow."

"You didn't have to do that, Ross."

"I know, but I wanted to. You're the only one I trust with the horses whenever I'm away." When he'd walked out of the suite after nearly making love to Celeste, Ross had strolled along the strip to find a shop selling musical instruments. He knew Jeremy played the harmonica, and he'd bought one and had it engraved with Jeremy's name.

"I'm heading back to my house—do you want me to drop you off at home?" he asked Jeremy. The vet's PTSD prevented him from driving, so every morning he walked the half mile to and from his sister's house to Ross's property.

"Thanks, but no thanks. I always feel better when I walk. If you don't mind, I'm going to hang out here until it's time to put the horses in for the night."

"Stay as long as you want, Jeremy."

Ross returned to the pickup and drove home. As he pulled into the driveway, he saw Celeste sitting on the front steps with Scamp on her lap.

"I gave him another bath," Celeste said, when he got out and approached her.

Ross folded his body down beside Celeste. "I've been told that Scamp has been sleeping here at night. Apparently, he's been waiting for you."

"That's because he wanted another spa treatment," she said.

"Wrong, Celeste. He wants you."

"That's because he knows I like him."

"I like you, too, and not because I want you to give me a bath."

"That's because you don't take baths."

"How do you do know?" Ross asked her.

"There's only a shower stall in the master bath, Ross."

"You've got me there," he said, chuckling. Celeste was right. He didn't take baths but wouldn't be opposed to sharing one with her.

"Now that he's sleeping here, we need to buy him a bed, Ross."

"I don't need to buy him a bed, Celeste. *You* need to buy him a bed. But before you get too close to that dog, we should take him to the vet to see if he's been microchipped."

Celeste gave him a direct stare. "And if he isn't? Then he can sleep here?"

A beat passed before Ross said, "Yes. He can sleep here."

Leaning closer, Celeste kissed his cheek. "Thank you, my love."

Ross smiled. "You're welcome."

"Oh, I forgot to tell you that Dean called to say the ratings for the interview went through the roof, and viewers want to see more of you."

"Will you be the one to interview me when we're ready?"

"Of course, Ross. I'm one of the network's sports reporters."

"Won't it smack of nepotism for a wife to interview her husband?"

"No. When we sit down together, I won't be in the role as your wife but a journalist."

"What if I decide to flirt with you?" Ross teased, smiling.

"It won't work because you wouldn't be the first athlete attempting to flirt, and I have a foolproof way of shutting them down."

Ross sobered and pressed a kiss on Celeste's hair. "I promise not to flirt or embarrass my wife."

"Thank you."

"When does he want you to submit the interview?"

"He wants it to air sometime next week."

"That means I'm going to have to give you a crash course on everything about the rodeo. Details you won't find on the internet."

Celeste blew out her cheeks. "How long do you think that will take?"

"No more than a couple of days." He knew she'd be a quick study. "You know, I'm actually looking forward to being interviewed by Celeste Burris."

Celeste shook her head. "Celeste Montgomery."

Ross went still. "You don't plan to change your name?"

"Legally I'm Burris, but professionally I'll still be Montgomery. Besides, it'll only be Burris for a short while."

Ross did not want to talk about Celeste leaving Bronco. He knew it was inevitable but still did not want to acknowledge it. "We'll begin discussing the rodeo Monday."

"I want to go into town Monday to shop for new clothes."

"Do you want me to take you?"

"No, thank you. I want to tour Bronco to familiarize myself with the businesses."

"Well, you should know there are two Broncos. There's Bronco Heights and Bronco Valley."

"Are you saying the Heights is for the hoity-toity, and the Valley for the common folks?" she teased, smiling.

Ross chuckled at her references. "I'd say the Valley is for the modest middle class while the more prosperous ranchers live in Bronco Heights. You should see some of those cattle ranches with thousands of acres of land. When folks mention the Abernathys, Taylors, or Daltons they're talking about the wealthiest families in Bronco."

"Are they like some rich families who will only marry within their social circle?"

"No. My brother's wife's sister is currently engaged to marry an Abernathy."

"How did that go over with the Abernathys?"

"Not only did they approve it, but they'd also devised a scheme to get Brynn and Garrett back together after their breakup."

"I have to assume it worked if they're now engaged."

"It did. And once Audrey and Corinne told me what they had planned after they got together with Garrett's brothers I couldn't stop laughing. It was ingenious."

"Tell me about it, Ross."

He shook his head. "No. If you ask one of them, I'm certain they'll share every duplicitous detail. You know, Audrey, Corinne, Brynn, and Remi are rodeo's Hawkins Sisters. If they're willing, you might want to interview them too." Ross saw Celeste's eyes light up with his suggestion. If the Hawkins Sisters agreed, it might extend Celeste's stay in Montana beyond May.

"Great idea, Ross. Now, not to change the subject, but is dinner with your family formal or casual?"

"Save your heels and power suits for the big city, Celeste. Around here, it's always casual. You're in boots and jeans country now." He grinned.

"I get it, Ross. If I'm married to a cowboy, then we should complement each other."

"You already accomplished that with our wedding because you were stunning. I nearly lost it when I walked into your suite and saw you in that gown."

Celeste rested her head on his shoulder. "All of this sweet talk is going to give me a big head."

"A word of warning, bae. I'm the only one in this family that is allowed to have a big head."

Her lips parted as she smiled.

"Does that mean we're on the same page?"

"I know exactly what you're talking about."

"Then you must know that you turn me on."

* * *

Celeste knew it was time she level with her husband.

"Yes, I was more than aware of that when you were on top of me. I was also turned on, Ross. But I'm glad we stopped when we did because that would've meant changing the guidelines, and that's not something I need."

"Need or want, Celeste?"

"Need *and* want, Ross. When our marriage is over, we should be able to pick up the pieces of our lives and move on."

"You keep bringing up going back to Chicago. Are you sure you don't have someone waiting there for you?"

She shook her head. "There hasn't been anyone in a couple of years."

"What happened?"

There was a notable silence before Celeste said, "He cheated on me. And not with just one woman. My friends kept hinting that he was creeping, but I didn't believe them until I saw it with my own eyes. He'd tried playing it off saying that the woman he was eating dinner with at our favorite restaurant was an old college friend, but I'd seen enough. She was practically sitting on his lap, and their body language said they were intimate. He began calling me at the station after I blocked his number. But when I refused to take his calls, he finally got the hint and stopped."

"Were you in love with him?"

"No. There were things I loved about him, but I can honestly say I wasn't in love with him."

"Would you have married him if he'd asked?"

"Probably," she said truthfully. "At that time, I wanted to be married because so many of my girlfriends were getting married. But after I broke up with DeAndre, I realized there were things I'd wanted to do and places I'd wanted to go, but I'd put them off because I was involved with him."

"What things?" Ross questioned.

Answering truthfully, Celeste was glad she could unburden herself. She was telling him things she hadn't told her mother when Sandra had questioned why she'd stopped seeing DeAndre.

"I want to travel to Europe, Asia, and Africa before I turn thirty-five."

"Why thirty-five?"

"That's when I figure my biological clock will begin ticking and I'll want children. If I don't have a baby before I'm forty, then I'll adopt. And being married isn't a prerequisite."

"You sound like a lady with a plan," Ross teased.

She raised her head and brushed a kiss over his mouth.

Ross turned to face Celeste and deepened the kiss at the same time Scamp growled and snapped at him. Pulling back, he glared at the dog. "Oh, hell no, traitor! There's no way I'm going to let you stay in my home if you're going to bite me."

"He's just trying to protect me," Celeste countered.

"Protect you from whom? Certainly not me."

She pulled Scamp closer to her chest. "You need to give him time to get used to you."

"What I'm going to give him is a one-way ticket to the Happy Hearts Animal Sanctuary so Daphne Cruise can put him up for adoption."

"No, you won't, Ross Burris. If you don't want Scamp, then I'll take him back to Chicago with me."

"He will never survive in a big city, Celeste, because he's used to being outdoors where he can run free and release energy."

Celeste stood up. "Make up your mind, Ross. You claim you want to put the dog up for adoption, but when I mention adopting him you beat your gums about where he should or should not live." Turning on her heel, Celeste went inside the house, leaving Ross sitting on the steps.

She set Scamp on the floor, and she followed the puppy to

the mudroom where she'd made a makeshift bed from one of her old sweatshirts and hunkered down next to him. "Don't worry, baby boy. You won't have to go to some old shelter as long I'm here." Scamp raised his head and emitted a soft woof.

Chapter Eight

Ross held the car door open for her when they left for his folks' house later that evening. "You can drive, and I'll navigate."

Celeste knew Ross was still upset about Scamp's growling and snapping at him. She didn't know why the puppy didn't like Ross, but that was something he had to work through with the canine. The housing complex where she'd purchased her town house allowed pets, but if she were to bring Scamp back to Chicago, she'd have to arrange for someone to look after him whenever she was on assignment.

She tapped the start engine button and programmed the nav system.

Ross fastened his own seat belt. "You remember their address?"

Celeste gave him a quick glance before backing out of the driveway. "It's a part of my job, Ross, to pay attention to details. I've trained myself to be an intent listener and observe everything when interviewing a subject."

"Impressive." His eyebrows rose as he nodded at her. "You know, I've been wondering… Why isn't there much personal data written about you on the internet?"

"Because that's the way I wanted it, Ross. I don't need someone hanging outside my home or flooding my personal email account with less than favorable comments about my appearance or reporting."

"But weren't you aware when you decided to go into broadcast journalism that you would or could become highly visible to the viewing public?"

"Yes. I have no control over the content the network approves for public viewing, but what I can control is my personal life. If I hadn't been able to do that, then we never would've been able to fool the public into believing our secret liaison."

"What about your friends?"

Celeste concentrated on her driving as she followed the map on the dashboard screen. "Some of them wanted to introduce me to other guys once I broke up with DeAndre, but I told them I wanted to take a break from dating."

Ross smothered a laugh. "It's apparent to them that your break did not include dating me."

"You're right about that because two of them sent me text messages asking that I call and tell them everything."

"Are you going to tell them?" Ross asked.

Celeste shook her head. "No. I'll just repeat the story the world knows about us." She blew out her breath. "You know, my parents would preach to me and my brothers that we always had to tell the truth, no matter how serious we thought something was, and it is something I've tried to do all my life. But now... I've become such an astute liar that I'm beginning to believe my own lies."

Ross knew what Celeste was feeling because he hated deceiving his parents about how he'd met Celeste. But what he hadn't lied to them about were his feelings for his wife. The cynical Ross Burris could've never imagined that he would fall for a woman within minutes of meeting her. He'd had relationships before, even one he'd thought of as serious, but what he felt for Celeste was different. So very different that when he'd devised the scenario that they marry, it had come from a place he hadn't known existed.

Ross had known from an early age what he'd wanted out of life. The media may have labeled him "charming and oozing sex appeal," but what they didn't see was his singular focus on achieving those goals. He'd lost track of the number of events in which he'd competed once he turned professional as he split his time between bronc riding and studying. And whenever he did take a break to date, and as his star rose in rodeo, so did his visibility whenever he was photographed with a woman.

Ross was aware that his life as a rodeo rider was not conducive to a stable relationship, and he was forthcoming when he'd admitted this to the women he dated. He hadn't understood that being candid with them would backfire with a litany of negative posts attacking his character.

His internal radar told him within seconds of meeting Celeste that she was different from any other woman he'd met. She didn't want to be photographed with him; she hadn't regarded him as an open wallet. And she couldn't care less that he was a celebrity because she was confident in herself, in her intelligence and professional training.

"Have you ever thought about what might have happened if we had met in Fort Worth? Would we have dated? Gotten married?" he asked Celeste.

"Believe it or not, I have Ross. It's probably because we do seem to get along well. Now, if you were to make up with Scamp, we could become one big happy family."

"Scamp and I will never be besties, Celeste. The dog just doesn't like me."

"That's because he feels you don't want him around."

"That's not true," Ross protested. "I happen to like dogs. But it could be a man thing."

"Why do you say that?"

"Jeremy said Scamp won't let him come close to him either."

Celeste turned into the horseshoe-shaped driveway, and

then parked behind his brothers' trucks. "Maybe Scamp prefers perfume to cologne."

Reaching for her right hand, Ross kissed the back of it. "The next time I shower I'll douse myself with your perfume."

"You don't douse perfume, Ross. You dab it on certain parts of the body."

He leaned closer. "I'm going to need a demonstration when you show me how you do it."

"Nah, nah, nah," Celeste drawled, shaking her head. "There's no way I'm going to let you see me without my clothes."

"You're naked when you dab on perfume? Damn!"

She unbuckled her belt. "Let's go, bae. I don't want your mother to blame me for making you late."

Ross unsnapped his belt. "Yeah, they'll probably believe we were busy doing you know what," he said, wiggling his eyebrows.

"They can believe whatever they want, but we know that's not going to happen."

He wanted to tell Celeste that he had changed his mind about that. That he had regretted including the no-sex rule in their deal. He realized he didn't want to sleep with her just because he was attracted to her but because he was developing strong feelings for her.

Whenever he came back to the house after cleaning the stalls, finding Celeste up and waiting for his return so they would share breakfast together shook him to his core. Her selfless act was more than enough for Ross to realize it was something he not only had begun to look forward to but wanted to last far beyond the month. He wanted to share breakfast, lunch, dinner, *and* a bed with his wife.

He helped Celeste out of the SUV and walked with her up to the house where he'd been raised and had experienced the most incredible childhood with his brothers and parents. When he opened the door Ross and Celeste were met with a chorus of congratulations and flashes from cell phone cameras.

Celeste wasn't given time to react before being lifted off her feet when Ross's brothers hugged her, and their women greeted her with kisses on her cheeks. Her face was burning when Benjamin picked up a bottle of chilled champagne, filled two flutes and handed them to her and Ross while the other Burrises picked up flutes off the buffet table in the dining room.

The Burris patriarch held up his glass. "To Ross and Celeste. We decided to surprise you because you more than shocked the hell of out of us when you decided to elope."

"Is there something you're not telling us, bro? Why you felt the need for a quickie wedding?" Mike called out.

Ross smiled. His brother had flown in from Chicago for the weekend before returning to med school to take finals. "Sorry to disappoint you, Mike, but Celeste and I are not ready to make you an uncle." Wrapping his free arm around Celeste's waist he met her eyes when she gave him a tentative smile. "Celeste, you've already met my parents, but I'd like to introduce you to Jack and his wife, Audrey." Jack raised his glass in acknowledgment. "Next to him is Mike and his fiancée, Corinne, who happens to be Audrey's sister."

"Geoff and Stephanie would be here if they weren't vacationing in Europe," Jeanne said.

Benjamin touched his flute to Ross's, then Celeste's. "I know I speak for everyone when I say, Celeste, welcome to the family. We're thrilled that the Burris clan grew by one more." Everyone echoed Benjamin's greeting as they touched glasses with one another.

Celeste took a sip of champagne, but she felt it lodge in her throat as she realized that over the next several weeks she would be interacting with this amazing family, sharing many more evenings together.

Guilt swept over her, swallowing her whole, and Celeste

was helpless to control the flood of tears welling up in her eyes. She'd just deceived—no, conned—Ross's family into believing she would be with them to celebrate weddings, births, and family holidays. She was nothing more than a fraud.

Ross stared at Celeste, not knowing what to do, because he'd always felt completely helpless whenever he saw a woman cry. Though he'd sat atop a one-ton bucking horse or jumped off one in full gallop to lasso a steer, right then he was unable to move.

Mike nudged him in the ribs. "Ross, take care of your wife."

He handed his younger brother his glass, and then gently pulled Celeste close. "It's okay, sweetheart. I know this is a little overwhelming for you."

"I'm sorry." Her apology was muffled in his shirt.

He dropped a kiss on her hair. "There's no need to apologize."

Corinne rested a hand on Ross's arm. "Let her go. Audrey and I will take care of Celeste."

Ross wanted to tell Mike's fiancée that as Celeste's husband he should be the one to take care of her, but decided it was best not to make a scene. "Okay." He watched as the three women left the room, wondering what had occurred to make Celeste emotional enough to cry. He'd witnessed variations of the speeches from his mother and father before and he'd watched as Stephanie, Audrey, and Corinne were brought to tears, but he hadn't expected the same reaction from Celeste.

He'd watched her deal with her overbearing boss, stare down failure, go along with a marriage charade, and crush a live TV interview. She'd even openly challenged him about a stray dog she had no intention of giving up. So why had she dissolved into tears when embraced by the family whose surname she now claimed?

* * *

Celeste, cloistered behind the bathroom door with Corrine and Audrey, blotted her eyes with a tissue. "I'm sorry about losing it."

Corinne waved a hand in a dismissive gesture. "Girl, please, there's no need to apologize. I went through the same ritual after Mike and I announced our engagement, and I cried so much that I wound up souping snot."

Audrey nodded. "Even though I told my sister what to expect, she still couldn't hold it together. And before you ask, I also got emotional."

Celeste sniffled, then blew her nose. "I'm embarrassed because I didn't even cry at my wedding."

Audrey handed Celeste another tissue. "Mothers and fathers cry at their children's wedding. A bride walking down the aisle crying sends the wrong message."

Now Celeste experienced even more guilt. She'd cheated her mother out of becoming the mother of the bride. She was Sandra's only daughter.

She took a quick glance in the mirror and groaned. "I look a hot mess."

Audrey pushed several strands of Celeste's hair behind her ear. "Don't say that. You look beautiful. I can see why Ross married you."

"And you were an incredibly beautiful bride," Corinne stated.

Celeste stared at her. "You saw the videos?"

Audrey nodded. "Of course. All of us are friends on social media and we were texting one another like crazy once they were uploaded to Ross's social platforms. Then Brynn called to tell us about your televised interview. She recorded it on DVR, and last night we went to the Flying A to watch it with her and Garrett. Everyone in Bronco is talking about Ross marrying a sports reporter. And I'm willing to bet there will be a lot of disappointed women in Montana once they realize that Ross Burris has exchanged his bachelor card for a wedding ring."

Corinne pointed to Celeste's hand. "Your ring is gorgeous."

"Thank you." And from the size of the diamonds in the rings on Audrey's and Corinne's hands there was no doubt the Burris men spared no expense on the women they loved. However, Celeste did not fool herself into believing Ross loved her, despite his public declaration. She jumped slightly when there came a knock on the door.

"Is Celeste, okay?" asked a familiar voice.

The three women shared a look. "She's okay, Ross," Audrey called out. "We were just coming out."

"It looks as if someone is worried about his wife," Corinne teased, smiling.

Celeste took one last look in the mirror. Her eyes were slightly puffy, but her waterproof mascara, as advertised, hadn't smeared. She opened the door and came face-to-face with Ross, his expression making it impossible for her to utter a word. It was an expression she assumed he seldom exhibited. Fear.

Was he afraid?

No, he couldn't be.

"I'm okay," she said softly.

He blinked once. "Are you sure?"

Celeste forced a smile. "Of course. I just got a little emotional."

Ross took her hand, giving it a gentle squeeze. "Geoff and Stephanie are on Zoom, and they want to meet you."

Celeste returned to the living room with the others and sat on a love seat with Ross facing the coffee table, where the Burrises had set a laptop. She waved to the images on the screen.

Geoff waved back. "Congratulations and welcome to the family. I heard you'd come to Bronco to interview me but wound up marrying my brother. Had you planned on that?"

Celeste smiled at the handsome rodeo superstar. "Not initially. Ross and I were seeing each other secretly for months, so when I got the assignment to come to Bronco to interview you and you were on vacation, we decided it was time to go public."

"So public that you decided to elope?" Stephanie asked, with a wide grin.

Celeste shared a look with Ross. "Yes. We both knew if we didn't do it now, then I didn't know when I'd get this much time off to be together again to plan a wedding."

"How long do you plan to stay in Montana?" Geoff questioned.

"Just until the end of the month. I'm going to do a few interviews and send them off to the station before I return to Chicago."

Stephanie leaned forward on her chair. "You're going to live in Chicago, while Ross is in Bronco?"

"It's only temporary. I'm still under contract to the network. Once that ends, then I'll move to Bronco."

"What say you, brother?" Geoff asked Ross.

Ross dropped an arm over Celeste's shoulders. "There's not much for me to say, because I was aware of Celeste's obligations once we decided to marry. It's not going to be much different from when we were dating. Whenever I wasn't competing, and she wasn't away on assignment we would get together at her place in Chicago."

Geoff nodded. "So, it looks as if you guys have worked out a deal."

"We have," Celeste and Ross said in unison.

"Congratulations to you both again. Hopefully Stephanie and I will get to meet you before you return to Chicago."

"Celeste, please show me your ring. Wow!" Stephanie gasped when Celeste put up her hand for her to see the eternity band. "Who picked it out?"

"It was Ross," Celeste admitted truthfully. And he had because she hadn't been able to make up her mind as to what she wanted.

"Nice going, Ross."

"Thank you, Stephanie," Ross countered, smiling.

"We're going to let you go because I know Mom's ready to serve dinner, and it's after midnight here. Congratulations again and much love to everyone."

The screen went dark, and Celeste felt as if she could breathe normally again. It was apparent she and Ross had survived the Burrises' inquisition unscathed. And again, Celeste marveled that she'd become a very adept liar. She and Ross gave award-winning performances. Ross even more so than she. The word *love* had slipped off his tongue so easily when she'd mentioned it in jest.

She smiled when Ross kissed her ear. "You know I could've interviewed Geoff on Zoom," she said sotto voce.

"And miss becoming Mrs. Ross Burris?" he teased. "Geoff wouldn't have agreed anyway. He and Stephanie wanted to relax and just enjoy each other. On the circuit they can go weeks without seeing each other." He passed his lips over her neck. "Mom is giving us the stink eye, so we'd better go into the dining room and join the rest of the family."

Family. Celeste had to acknowledge that the Burrises were indeed now her family because she was legally married to Ross. What a mess she'd made of her life. She had lied to the public, to Ross's family, and to her parents. And she wondered when the lies would stop, because now that she'd told one lie, she would be forced to tell another, and then another until she didn't know what was real or make-believe.

I hope I don't break character before this charade is over. I'm living in an imaginary world that if discovered could ruin everything I've worked so hard to achieve.

Celeste's traitorous thoughts attacked her like sharp needles poking her exposed flesh. She rubbed her arms vigorously.

"Are you okay?" Ross whispered close to her ear.

She lowered her arms and stared straight ahead, knowing if she looked at him, she wouldn't be able to hide her feelings. "I'm fine."

"You don't look fine, Celeste."

She forced a smile that did not reach her eyes. "I'm still overwhelmed about meeting your family."

"We can be a handful when all of us get together, but I can assure you we're harmless."

"I know that, Ross. I like your family."

"Our family," he corrected softly.

She nodded. It was a possessive adjective she had to get used to for the duration of her abbreviated marriage to a man with whom she'd feared she was falling in love.

There was nothing about Ross she did not love. She'd found him to be kind and patient, even with his fans. He was more than generous, paying for her ring and her wedding attire despite her protests. He was effusive when he thanked her for getting up early to prepare breakfast for him, and shrugged off her excuse that she, too, had to eat.

Although she and Ross were playing a game and playing it very well, she didn't want it to end with May. She wanted a tie game that would require overtime.

"Yes. Our family," she said. Then she took his hand, and they entered the dining room.

"Who do you intend to interview while you're here?" Audrey asked Celeste, once they were seated and had filled their plates.

She swallowed a mouthful of delicious honey-glazed ham before saying, "I'd like to interview you and your sisters for a featured weekend segment."

Audrey and Corinne exchanged looks. "You're going to have to wait for us to get back, because the Hawkins Sisters are booked up for the next two months. We plan to be back in time for the Bronco Summer Family Rodeo that's held during the Fourth of July celebration."

Corinne set down her water glass. "You may be able to catch up with our older sister, Brynn, before you leave because she's going to be sitting out some of the events on the circuit. Right now, she's concentrating on going into business, selling quilts and handmade needlecrafts."

Ross rested a hand on Celeste's arm. "I'll call Brynn to find out if she's willing to be interviewed, and if she is then you two can coordinate a time when she's available."

Celeste's confidence was renewed when she thought about the possibility of interviewing a woman rodeo rider. "Thank you, my love." The endearment had slipped out unconsciously and his family exchanged knowing smiles.

"Anytime," Ross whispered. Leaning to his left, he dropped a kiss on her hair.

"You two need to get a room," Mike teased.

"We have a room. In fact, our house has lots of rooms, little brother."

"Do you plan on turning one of those rooms into a nursery?" Jack asked.

Jeanne held up her hand. "That's enough. Y'all must respect Ross and Celeste's privacy. I'm certain they'll let us know when they're ready to start a family."

Ross applauded. "Thank you, Mom, for shutting down these wannabe detectives."

Celeste also wanted to applaud Ross's mother because when it came to the topic of her having Ross's baby it was a nonstarter. For her to get pregnant, they would have to have sex.

Dinner ended with coffee and dessert and Celeste was grateful Ross volunteered to drive home because not only was she full but exhausted from getting up early for them to board their flight back to Montana.

Scamp was waiting for them when Ross drove up.

"Are you going to let him sleep in the house?" she asked Ross.

"Why are you asking me when he's your dog and this is your house, Celeste?"

Turning her head, she hid a smile. "Just checking."

"Yeah, right," he drawled, shutting off the engine. He got out of the vehicle and came around to assist Celeste.

Even though she'd married Ross, she didn't want to make assumptions that would put them at odds with each other. They'd concocted a scheme as a couple so hopelessly in love that they'd eloped for a quickie marriage. If they disagreed it had to occur behind closed doors and be resolved before going out together in public. They could smile and pretend all was right, but it was almost impossible to disguise body language. And Celeste had no intention of falling prey to some reporter or photographer looking to uncover their deception.

"I'm going to see Scamp settled for the night, then I'm going to turn in."

Ross took a step and kissed her forehead. "Good night."

She nodded. "Good night." And headed to her bed. Alone.

Chapter Nine

Celeste woke early Saturday morning to the sound of rain tapping against the windows. Turning over, she buried her face in the mound of pillows cradling her shoulders. Even though she wanted to go back to sleep she knew she had to get up and take care of Scamp.

Twenty minutes later, after making her bed, showering, and dressing, she walked out of her bedroom to see that Ross had left his door open. Before leaving for Vegas, she'd noticed that he'd always closed it. She peered inside to find the bed unmade.

"Are you looking for me?"

She turned and saw Ross smiling at her. He'd come up the stairs so quietly that she hadn't heard his approach. "Yes and no."

"It's either yes or no, Celeste."

Celeste felt as if she'd been ensnared in a force field from which there was no escape. That the man she'd married had woven a sensual spell over her.

"It's both, Ross. It's the first time that I noticed you did not close your bedroom door."

Ross stared at her under lowered lids. "There's no need for me to close the door now that we're married. I don't want to put up barriers that'll make it difficult for us to feel comfortable with each other."

"What about my door?"

"That's your choice."

She nodded. "Okay. I was going down to take care of Scamp."

"Don't worry about him. I let him out and when he came back, I gave him water."

"What about the horses?"

"I'm going to keep them in the stable until the threat of thunderstorms is over. What's on your agenda today?"

"After breakfast, I'll do some laundry and later this afternoon I plan to go online to read the comments about our interview before I outline the stories I plan to send to the network."

"While you do that, I'm going to call the animal hospital to see if I can get an appointment for Scamp."

"How are you going to do that when he won't let you pick him up?" Celeste questioned.

"No longer a problem. Your fur baby and I had a man-to-man talk this morning. I told him if he wants to live here, then he can't go around growling and biting the hand that feeds him. I must have gotten through to him because he let me pick him up."

Celeste couldn't stop smiling. "I'm glad you two made up."

"I'm glad you're glad. Now I'm going down to make breakfast for us."

"What's on the menu?"

"Shrimp and grits."

"You're kidding?"

Ross shook his head. "Nope. I could eat shrimp and grits for breakfast, lunch, and dinner."

When Celeste had taken inventory of his freezer, she saw several bags of frozen shrimp, catfish filets, and salmon. It was apparent he was serious about learning to cook fish. "Would you like a sous chef?"

He dropped a kiss on her hair. "Yes, please."

I know I shouldn't get too used to this. Because not only do I know how this is going to end, I doubt if I'll be able to become involved with another man and experience what I have with Ross.

Celeste knew it was Ross's laid-back personality that had made it so easy for her to get along with him. And what she liked was that he wasn't into playing head games. He was outspoken and that was what the women he'd dated were unable to accept. However, Celeste expected that in a relationship. She hadn't wanted to analyze double messages or second-guess what was being said.

Sharing the kitchen with Ross as they prepared breakfast was what she'd looked forward to experiencing over and over and not just for the month of May but for many more years of Mays to come.

They'd lingered over several cups of coffee listening to prerecorded music coming from hidden speakers Ross had synched with the playlist on his cell phone. She'd discovered he had an eclectic taste in music that ranged from country to cool jazz and R & B. He had even included a few movie soundtracks.

Ross had called the local animal hospital and managed to get an appointment for Scamp, and Celeste took advantage of his absence to put up a couple of loads of laundry after she'd emptied the hampers in both bathrooms and changed the linen on Ross's bed. She then cleaned all the bathrooms. She'd finished dusting, vacuuming, and had taken a whole chicken out of the freezer to defrost when Ross returned with Scamp.

Ross set three large shopping bags on the floor. "I think I bought everything you'll need for Scamp, including a few chew toys so hopefully he won't start gnawing on chair and table legs. Scamp isn't chipped, so when I filled out the paperwork, I listed you as Scamp Burris's owner. The vet said he's about three months old and quite healthy given that he was a stray. He got a series of shots, so he may be a little lethargic for a day or two."

Bending over, Celeste gently scratched the puppy behind

his ears as he lay on the floor, eyes closed. "Do you hear that, baby boy? No one will ever call you a stray again. You're officially Scamp Burris." She pointed to the shopping bags. "What else did you buy besides chew toys?"

"Food and water bowls, wee-wee pads, a couple of beds, dry and canned puppy food—"

"Enough, Ross," Celeste interrupted, laughing. "What did you do? Buy out the store?"

"I did get a kennel that I have to put together. He may feel more secure sleeping in the mudroom in an enclosure because he's used to sleeping in one of the stalls."

"Thank you, Ross."

"For what?"

"For taking care of Scamp."

He smiled. "He's a Burris, sweetheart, and I don't ever want you to forget that we always look after one another."

"And if I do forget, I'm certain you'll remind me."

"You know I will." He sniffed the air. "Why do I smell pine?"

"That's because I cleaned the bathrooms."

Ross frowned. "I don't want you cleaning when you could be doing other things. You asked me to give the housekeeper the month off, and I did, but that doesn't mean you have to take over for her."

"I don't intend to argue with you," she said, glaring at him. "I'm not some prima donna who believes she's too good to clean a bathroom or push a vacuum cleaner. I don't have the luxury of hiring someone to clean my condo. I also happen to know how to use a washer and dryer, so when you go upstairs to your bedroom, you'll find that I also did your laundry. So, are you going to have a beef with me because I changed your bed and emptied your hamper?"

Ross ran a hand over his face. He hadn't meant to bark at Celeste, but he didn't want her to spend her free time cleaning a house—a house that was too large for two people. "No, bae, I'm not going have beef with you."

"Then what's your problem?" she countered.

"My problem is I know you're here to work and not clean." He held up a hand when she opened her mouth. "Please let me finish. It may surprise you, but I know how to turn on the washer, dryer, and dishwasher, so you're exempt from doing laundry and dishes."

Celeste gave him a direct stare. "What if we compromise?"

Something told Ross that the woman he'd married wasn't going to concede so easily, because she'd challenged him about Scamp, and in the end, she'd come out the winner. She had her dog. "What are you proposing?"

"I'll do the laundry and clean the bathrooms, while you dust and vacuum. We can share cooking and cleaning the kitchen. I'll take care of Scamp, while you continue caring for the horses."

"A division of labor," he said with a smile.

A hint of a smile tilted the corners of her mouth, drawing his gaze to linger there. Ross never tired of seeing her smile or sitting across from her to watch her eat while he'd fantasized kissing her mouth—over and over until both were left breathless.

"Okay, then. I'll agree to that."

Her smile broadened and it was dazzling. "Thank you."

Ross shook his head. "No, Celeste. Thank you."

"For what?"

"For being here. For agreeing to spend the month with me. I never realized how empty this house felt before you came to live here."

"Are you saying that you were lonely?" she asked.

Her question gave Ross pause. He recalled the times that he'd come home after competing to encounter complete silence. There was no one or nothing to greet him when he opened the door. Most times he'd been too hyped up or exhausted to want to do anything other than take a shower and crawl into bed. He'd taken possession of the house in December and other than the women in his family, Celeste was the first woman he'd invited into his home.

"No," he admitted, shaking his head. "I've never felt lonely, because I have my family. And my decision to live here alone was by choice."

"You were alone until Scamp and I came along to disrupt your well-ordered existence."

Ross angled his head. "I don't think of you and Scamp as disruptions. Both of you are what I need to remind me there is life outside of the rodeo."

"What about your after-school program, Ross? I'm certain once that's up and running and you're competing part-time, you'll be so busy that you'll be forced to hire a social secretary."

"I doubt if it will come to that. I plan to have a staff of volunteers to help the students."

"Have you finalized the prospectus?" Celeste asked him.

"Yes. Before we sit down for you to interview me, I'll show you everything, including the abandoned building I bought in downtown Bronco Valley."

"I can't believe I'm married to a schoolteacher cowboy."

Ross knew Celeste would be more than surprised—perhaps even shocked if she'd known the depth of his feelings for her. That he liked her, liked being married to her, liked having her live with him, and liked her sharing her life with him.

"What you see is what you get, sweetheart."

"That's what I like about you, Ross."

He didn't have enough time to tell Celeste what he liked about her. "And I like you, Celeste. I like you so much more than I should because we both know how this is going to end."

"You're right. We're exceptional because we knew even before exchanging vows that our marriage would be short-lived.

We've become actors in a scripted reality show that will never be televised."

A beat passed. "What if we decided to do away with the script?" he asked Celeste.

Her eyelids fluttered as she shook her head. "No, Ross. I'm in Bronco because of an assignment I must complete by the end of the month. I'm not going to lie and say I'm not going to miss you or your family, but I've worked too hard to secure my position at the station to let personal sentiment derail the plans I've made for my future. And I know it's the same for you."

"You're right, but other than securing your position with your network where do you see yourself in another five to ten years? Do you still plan to continue to travel on assignment?"

"No, Ross. Ultimately, I want to become a baseball commentator for a major league team. I'm willing to bet that I know as much or even more baseball statistics going back centuries than some of the more popular commentators."

Ross stared at Celeste, complete surprise freezing his features. "Really?"

She smiled. "Yes, really. I have an incredible memory when it comes to numbers. I can quote the batting averages of practically every player in the Negro Leagues and on the Chicago White Sox."

"The White Sox and not the Cubs?"

She lowered her eyes. "I live in Auburn Gresham, known to locals as Gresham, which is located on the far side of the South Side of Chicago, so I'm a White Sox fan. What I will admit is that I like Wrigley Field because the ivy-covered brick outfield wall gives the ballpark more character than the former Comiskey Park which is now Guaranteed Rate Field. You know, Comiskey Park was the site of the heavyweight title match in which Joe Louis defeated then champion James Braddock in eight rounds."

"You truly are a font of sports knowledge."

"Most sports, with rodeo being the exception," Celeste admitted.

Ross smiled at her. "That's going to change when I teach you about the sport. Meanwhile I'm going to put the kennel together, then drive over to let the horses out for a few hours now that it's no longer raining."

"And I'm going to check on the chicken that's defrosting for tonight's dinner."

"Save the chicken for tomorrow. I'd like to take you to Doug's. It's what you'd call a dive bar and a popular hangout for those living in Bronco. The food is good, and the beers are cold."

"That sounds like my kind of place."

"So, the city girl is looking to get an infusion of country?" he teased.

Celeste scrunched up her nose. "The only thing I'm going to say is watch me."

Ross wanted to tell her that was all he'd been doing since watching her walk into DJ's Deluxe.

As soon as they entered Doug's, Celeste was met with voices raised in conversations to be heard over the music coming from a colorful jukebox. There was a crowd at the bar standing two deep and it appeared as if every booth and table was occupied.

Celeste glanced up at Ross, every inch the cowboy in jeans, boots, and a white T-shirt under a denim jacket. He touched the brim of his Stetson to acknowledge those who slapped his back as they congratulated him on his recent marriage. Mouthwatering aromas wafted to her nostrils when waitstaff, balancing trays on their shoulders, wended their way through the crowd.

"Let's see if we can find a table toward the back," Ross said in her ear.

She nodded. It wasn't six o'clock and if she'd been in Chicago, it would've been the time when happy hour was winding down. Whenever she was in town, she'd made it a practice to hang out with her colleagues after work several times a month. It had been their time to bitch and moan about what was going on in the office, and they'd sworn an oath never to repeat it to anyone outside the group or they would vehemently deny who said it.

Even though she and Dean were engaged in an undeclared war where he'd wanted to micromanage every phase of her reporting, she was careful not to bring up his name in conversation because she did not want to inflame their less than amicable working relationship.

Handing in her assignments on time and not openly challenging him in staff meetings did little to decelerate his attempt to get rid of her, though. One of the meteorologists had confided to her that Dean was interested in dating her but had changed his mind after a producer had lost his job when several women had complained about him sexually harassing them and sued the network. Whatever the reason for Dean's behavior, Celeste was determined to stick it out and make a name for herself.

Ross placed a hand on her lower back, interrupting her thoughts. He led her over to a table for two in a far corner near the kitchen.

Before he sat, he beckoned a waitress close as she headed for the kitchen. "Do you still have chili?"

The young woman flashed a sexy grin. "I'm certain I can find some for you."

Ross lowered his head, smiling. "Thanks."

She winked at him. "Anytime, cowboy."

Celeste gave him a direct stare when he sat opposite her. "Does this happen all the time?"

"What are you talking about?"

"Women flirting with you."

"Nah, bae. She was just trying to be friendly."

"I'm certain she saw the ring on your hand, or did she choose to ignore it?"

"Where is all of this coming from? No wait," he said, leaning over the table. "Are you jealous?"

"Of course not," she said quickly.

Ross leaned back and shook his finger. "Something tells me you are, and that means what you feel for me is a little more than liking."

"Now you're being ridiculous, Ross, because even though she saw me sitting here she had no shame about disrespecting me by flirting with my husband."

"Oh, so it's about overstepping because we're married."

"Duh! Yes, Ross. Would you like it if dudes totally ignored you and came on to me?"

"They wouldn't dare."

"And why not?"

"Because they know I'd knock them on their asses."

Celeste's jaw dropped. "You want to fight dudes but…" Her words trailed off when a tall, slender woman with curls flowing down her back launched herself at a grinning Ross.

To say the woman was beautiful was an understatement. Waves of jealousy, which Celeste had just denied, washed over her when she was able to glimpse a sprinkling of freckles over the pert nose and cheeks of the woman's café au lait complexion. Not again, she thought. The first time she'd been thoroughly embarrassed was when she'd caught her boyfriend in an intimate embrace with a woman in a restaurant, and now it was her husband with a woman in a restaurant filled with people who knew him.

Smiling, Ross stood and curved an arm around the woman's waist. "Celeste, I'd like you to meet Brynn Hawkins. Brynn, my wife, Celeste Burris."

Celeste was grateful for her darker complexion to conceal

the blush when she realized she'd made a mental faux pas. She extended her hand to Brynn. "It's nice meeting you."

Brynn ignored the proffered hand and hugged Celeste. "Same here. When my sisters called me, they couldn't stop talking about you."

Ross rested a hand on Brynn's shoulder. "Are you here alone?"

"No. Garrett's parking the truck."

He smiled at Celeste. "Would you mind if Brynn and Garrett join us?"

She wanted to ask Ross if he was kidding. When he'd mentioned contacting Brynn Hawkins for an interview, Celeste did not think she would meet the rodeo rider this soon. "Of course not."

"I think I see some people getting up from a booth," he said. "Wait here and I'll ask the waitress to clean the table for us."

Brynn turned and smiled at Celeste. "So, I've heard that you and Ross eloped. If Ross Burris was willing to put a ring on your finger, then you must be very special."

"Why would you say that?" Celeste asked Brynn.

"I never believed all those reprehensible comments posted about him on social media because once I met Jeanne and Benjamin Burris, I knew they hadn't raised their sons to mess over women. And I saw how Jack and Mike treated my sisters with love and respect."

"I don't know if this is the right time, but I'd like to ask you if I could interview you for a piece I'm doing on the rodeo. I'd love to get a woman's perspective on the sport. And you would be perfect as one of the Hawkins Sisters."

Brynn smiled. "Of course. I won't be joining my sisters on the circuit until the end of the month. Give me your number, and we can set up a date and time to meet at the Flying A."

Celeste was slightly taken aback by Brynn's suggestion.

"You want to conduct the interview at your fiancé's family's ranch?"

"Yes. Garrett and I are living together and there is a building on the property where I do my needlecrafting when I'm not competing. I'd like people to see that rodeo stars have lives outside of the arena."

"Thank you, Brynn." She'd found herself saying those two words a lot since coming to Bronco, because everyone seemed so amenable and gracious.

She saw a tall man coming in their direction and when he dipped his head to kiss Brynn, Celeste knew he had to be Garrett Abernathy. There was something no-nonsense about the wealthy rancher, but judging from the way he stared at Brynn, Celeste knew he was hopelessly in love with his obviously younger fiancée.

Brynn made the introductions and Celeste felt the warmth of Garrett's smile when he cradled her hand in his. And judging from the calluses on his palm he was no stranger to hard work.

Brynn looped her arm through Garrett's. "Celeste is going to come out to the ranch to interview me for a piece she's doing for television."

"That's great," Garrett said, smiling. "Do you ride, Celeste?"

She grimaced. "Not really."

"I'm sure Brynn will give you a few lessons, and then we'll also show you around the ranch so you can see the cattle and bison."

"You actually have bison?" she asked Garrett.

He nodded. "Yes."

Celeste could not have imagined when Dean banished her to Montana to interview Geoff Burris that it would turn into such an adventure. "I'm really looking forward to seeing them."

"I'll arrange for you and Ross to stay overnight because you won't be able to see everything in one day."

"Garrett's right. Once we confirm a date, prepare to spend the night."

"Our table is ready," Ross said, as he rejoined them.

"Ross, Garrett and I want you and Celeste to spend the night at our place on the ranch when she comes to interview me," Brynn told Ross.

Ross turned his head in seemingly slow motion when he looked at Brynn, then at Celeste. "Okay."

Celeste felt her heart beating so fast that she feared it could be seen though her sweater. If she and Ross were to spend the night on the Flying A, then there was no doubt they would be expected to share a bed.

Suck it up, Celeste. You're supposed to be a grown-ass woman. You can't punk out because you'll sleep in the same bed as your husband.

Celeste hoped it would be the first and last obstacle she would have to face until it came time for her to leave Bronco. But something told that it would only be the beginning.

Chapter Ten

Surrounded by the noise of the crowd at Doug's, Celeste listened intently as Brynn told her about how the Hawkins Sisters had performed in Bronco's Summer Family Rodeo and then later that fall with the Burris Brothers at the Mistletoe Rodeo, and that's when she met the Abernathys.

"I liked Garrett even though there were rumors that he didn't date."

"Bad breakup or marriage?" Celeste asked.

"He'd married his high school sweetheart and they'd lived in New York for ten years before they divorced, and he came back to Bronco. We began dating and I thought everything was going well but Garrett said he was too old for me and called it quits. He was forty-three was I was thirty."

"Stop it!" Celeste drawled. "That's only a thirteen-year difference."

"As far as he was concerned it could have been thirty years. I also had an issue because he refused to talk about his ex-wife, and I wasn't about to plan a future with a man not willing to let go of the past."

"So, you both had issues?"

"Yes. I was more than willing to move on, but my sisters and Garrett's brothers decided to stage an intervention to get us back together."

"What did they do?" Celeste whispered.

"Do you recall seeing the music video with Derrick Blackstone when he covered Adele's 'Don't You Remember?'"

Celeste rolled her eyes upward. "Oh my gosh. Talk about sexy." The video had earned Blackstone a Grammy nomination.

"Well, I was the woman in the video."

"You're kidding?"

Brynn smiled. "No. I looked different because of the hair and makeup, but that was me. The video dropped a few days later and the meddling Hawkinses and Abernathys got together and told Garrett that I was going to hook up with Blackstone at the Houston Livestock Show and Rodeo where dozens of country stars were on the program."

"Were you scheduled to compete?"

Brynn shook her head. "No, but Garrett didn't know that when his brother showed him the video. He knew about Blackstone's reputation for sleeping with lots of women and he was afraid that if I did get involved with the man, then we'd never get back together. He came to my apartment and bared his soul about his marriage and divorce, while I told him I'd had enough of rodeo cowboys and celebrity types." She paused as a blush darkened her complexion. "The makeup sex was incredible. A couple of days later he gave me an emerald and diamond promise ring, then surprised me with the diamond for Valentine's Day."

"You're living a true Cinderella story," Celeste whispered.

"And you're not, Celeste?" Brynn countered. "You managed to get one of rodeo's superstars to fall in love and marry you. There was a time when Ross was called the Tom Jones of rodeo because women were throwing their panties into the arena after he'd performed."

"I didn't know that." In fact, Celeste had known very little about the rodeo rider other than his bad boy reputation. "I see Ross and Garrett coming this way. And as I said before, everything you just told me is off the record." Although Brynn had been forthcoming about her relationship with Garrett, Celeste knew her relationship with Ross would remain their secret in perpetuity.

Ross and Garrett set four frosty mugs of beer on coasters. "We put in an order for four chili burgers and fries," Ross said, as he sat close to Celeste. "Doug's chili burgers are phenomenal."

Garrett raised his mug, the others at the table following suit. "All the best to Ross and Celeste as you begin your new life together. Remember that love is the beginning of a life-long romance."

Celeste smiled as everyone touched glasses before taking a swallow of the cold brew, and wondered how many more toasts she would become a participant in before leaving Bronco. It was forty minutes later when the music stopped, and a hush fell over the assembly as a man cleared his voice.

"Good folks, it has come to my attention that one of Bronco's celebrities has been holding out on us. Ross Burris, can you and your lovely bride please stand up so we can celebrate with you properly? Someone who lives on a ranch in Bronco Heights, and whose name I will not disclose—but it begins with an *A*—has been generous enough to pay for a round of drinks for everyone." He paused. "Thank you for your generosity, Garrett Abernathy." Laughter, stomping, and applause followed the announcement.

Garrett lowered his head. "So much for anonymity," he said under his breath.

Ross cupped Celeste's elbow and eased her to stand while hooting and whistling seemed to shake the building's foundation and she buried her face against his shoulder. Then came the distinctive sound of tapping against glass and Celeste had attended enough weddings to know that it was the signal for the groom to kiss his bride.

Ross smiled at her. "You know what this means."

"Yes," she whispered. The word was barely off her tongue when Ross covered her mouth in a possessive kiss that weakened her knees so much, she had to hold on to his jacket to keep her balance.

What happened next became a blur as people who knew Ross came over to congratulate him; some gave him shot glasses of amber liquid which he tossed back, grinning. She managed to get him to eat his burger and some fries before he tossed back more shots.

"No more!" she told a man holding a filled shot glass in each hand. "Please. He's had enough."

"I'm good," Ross said.

"No, you're not good, Ross. Are you aware of how many shots you had?"

He flashed a lopsided grin. "Four?"

"Try twice that much. We're going home, and I'm driving." Celeste stood. "Garrett and Brynn, I'm sorry but I need to get Ross home."

Garrett pushed to his feet. "Do you need help getting him outside?"

"I don't think so." Ross was steady on his feet as she steered him out of the bar and to his pickup. He didn't protest when he sat on the passenger seat, and she fastened his seat belt.

"Do you know how to get back?" he asked when she started the engine.

"Please don't say anything to me until we get home, Ross."

"Are you angry with me, bae?"

"No, Ross. I'm just annoyed."

"That's better." The two words were followed by a soft snore.

He was still asleep when she tapped the remote device to the garage door. Once she parked, Celeste shook Ross to wake him. He grunted but didn't move. There was no way she was going to be able to move a man weighing more than two hundred pounds from the truck and into the house.

She shook him again, this time harder. "Ross, wake up."

He opened his eyes. "What?"

"You've got to get out and go inside." Leaning to her right, she unsnapped his belt. "Don't move until I come around and open the door."

Celeste managed to get Ross out of the truck without him falling and supported him up the staircase and into his bedroom where he fell face down on the bed. She knew she had to get him undressed, but that would have to wait until she took care of Scamp.

Scamp was in his kennel asleep. She let him out to do his business, then refilled his water bowl, dimmed the light in the mudroom, and went back upstairs to see if Ross had stirred.

Celeste turned on the bedside lamp and put her face close to Ross's. "Baby, you're going to have to wake up and help me get you undressed."

She must have gotten through to him because he turned over on his back, groaning as if in pain. "It serves you right if you wake up with a bitch of a hangover," she said, as she removed his boots and socks. Celeste continued her chastising monologue as she removed his jacket and belt, and then struggled to pull his jeans off his hips and down his legs. She was breathing heavily when he lay there sprawled on the bed in a white T-shirt and black boxer briefs, one muscled arm thrown above his head. Celeste picked up the lightweight blanket from the foot of the bed when without warning his eyes opened, and he stared at her, unblinking.

"What happened?"

She smiled. "You don't remember?"

"I remember drinking beer at Doug's."

"It wasn't the beer, Ross. You were downing shots whenever someone came over to congratulate you on our marriage," she explained as she spread the blanket over his lower body.

He groaned. "How many did I have?"

"I think it was around eight. Good thing you had me as the designated driver."

Ross mumbled a curse under his breath, then patted the mattress. "Stay with me, bae."

Celeste shook her head. "No, Ross. If you want, I can brew you a cup of coffee."

"I don't need coffee. I need my wife to stay with me. Only for a little while," he said after a pregnant pause. "Please, Celeste."

She found Ross's plea to stay with him vaguely disturbing. Did he know what he was asking? Did he want them to do more than sleep together? "Okay, Ross. But I'm going to have to change my clothes."

He'd closed his eyes again. "I'll be here waiting for you."

She walked across the hall and into her bedroom to change into a pair of cotton pajamas.

As expected, Ross was asleep when she slipped into the bed beside him. He looped an arm over her waist but did not wake up. It took Celeste fifteen minutes before she was able to relax enough to fall asleep.

Ross's internal clock woke him at five and he glanced over at the slender body beside him. His head ached, and his mouth felt as if it was filled with cotton, and then he remembered everything. Downing congratulatory shots at Doug's, Celeste driving back to the house, and then undressing him. But what he didn't recall was her getting into bed with him. He ran a hand over his face. Had he been that drunk that she had to monitor him?

He got out of bed without waking her and walked to the ensuite bath. After brushing his teeth, gargling with mouthwash, and splashing cold water on his face he felt as if he was partially ready to leave the house for his morning chores.

Ross found the clothes he'd worn the night before folded neatly on a chair and put them on. When he saw his boots under the chair, he realized he really must have been out of it because he would've left them on the shoe rack in the mudroom.

Never again, he swore.

Ross hadn't been a traditional college student living or attending classes on campus, so he hadn't attended frat parties where kegs of beer and beer pong games were commonplace. And there had never been a time when he was of legal age that he'd overindulged. What he couldn't understand was why at twenty-six, soon to be twenty-seven, he had reverted to behavior attributed to someone in his teens.

Not only had karma come for a visit, but this time she was accompanied by her aunties. Because it was the first time he'd been given the opportunity to share a bed with his wife and he hadn't been aware she lay beside him until he woke.

Scamp was out of his kennel and waiting for him when he walked into the mudroom. The puppy appeared more animated than he had the day before. Ross put the harness and lead on Scamp and led him outside. Now that he was a house dog, he had to get used to verbal commands. Ten minutes later he led Commander out of his stall. He washed and rinsed the stallion and turned him loose to graze. Blizzard, Belle, Traveler, and Domino underwent the same routine as Scamp trotted after them while Ross mucked out the stalls. The sun had pierced the veil of low-hanging clouds by the time he returned to the house. The rain that swept over Bronco had chased away the unusual warm spring temperatures, dropping them from seventy to forty.

Scamp returned as he started up the pickup, whining. Ross got out and set the puppy on a blanket on the rear seats and secured his leash to keep him from falling. It'd only taken two days for the dog to abandon hanging out with the horses and decide he wanted to become a house pet.

When he opened the door to the mudroom, Ross knew Celeste was up because she'd changed the wee-wee pads and filled the water dish. He took off his boots and made his way into the kitchen.

Celeste met Ross's eyes when he walked into the kitchen, and she handed him a mug of steaming coffee. "It's black," she said, then turned her back. She knew he liked his coffee with a splash of cream, but this morning called for a hangover beverage.

"Good morning, Celeste."

She turned to glare at him. "Is it really, Ross?"

He nodded. "It is because you knew enough not to let me drive home after I had a few."

"A few, Ross? Really. You had so many I lost count."

He took another sip before grimacing. "I've never done shots before, not even in my teens." Before she could reply, he added, "I'm sorry, Celeste. I didn't mean to embarrass you."

"I got you out of Doug's before you embarrassed the both of us."

Ross shook his head. "It will never happen again."

"I know it won't, Ross, because the next time you're on your own."

"You're a hard woman, Celeste Burris."

"I thought you said you were the only one in this family to get hard," she retorted.

He smiled and in that instant Celeste knew she could not remain annoyed with him. That he'd been a good sport and had accepted the congratulatory shots the same way he'd patiently signed autographs for his fans.

His smile faded. "How did you wind up in my bed?"

"You don't remember? You asked me not to leave you. That

you needed your wife to stay with you. Was that you or the liquor talking?"

Ross shook his head. "I don't know. There are some things about last night that are still a little hazy."

"You don't remember me undressing you?"

"Nope."

"It took me a while, but I did manage it. You must know that you're not a lightweight." She'd never tell him how it affected her, seeing him in nothing but boxer briefs that revealed his muscled thighs and a T-shirt that molded to his abs. Just thinking about it had her flushed. "You have twenty minutes to clean up before we sit down to breakfast."

Ross sniffed under both arms. "I do smell a little rancid."

"You smell like hay and manure. Now, please get out of my kitchen so I can finish making breakfast."

"What's on this morning's menu?"

"Oatmeal."

"Don't you mean oatmeal bread or cookies?"

"No. It's oatmeal with fruit. You need something that won't upset your stomach." Celeste waved her hand. "Now go."

I sound like a wife. And I'm acting like a wife because I'm concerned about his well-being. How has it happened so quickly? How have I morphed into the role within days of exchanging vows? Either I'm a better actress than I could've ever imagined, or this is something I wanted within minutes of falling under Ross Burris's charming spell.

What Celeste did not want to do was second-guess herself when it came to her relationship with Ross. Yes, he was her husband, albeit temporarily, but she wondered how long she could pretend that she was unaffected by his very presence. Whenever he touched her, kissed her, or smiled at her she was certain he knew what she was thinking and feeling. The sexual tension had begun to get to her when she'd begun having erotic dreams in which Ross was making love to her. She woke, shaking and waiting for the pulsing between her legs to subside. And when it did Celeste was left even more frustrated.

Ross retreated to the family room after breakfast to watch television. He alternated watching the Cowboy Channel, featuring rodeos in various cities, and CMT—Country Music Television.

Celeste had been unusually quiet during breakfast, and he decided not to initiate conversation because he knew she was still processing what had happened the night before. Ross had had no idea when he had ordered beer from the bar that Garrett had given one of the bartenders enough money to pay for a round of drinks for everyone in Doug's to celebrate Ross's marriage. It had come as a surprise to Ross and a shock to Celeste. What he hadn't anticipated was people offering him celebratory shots of Doug's best whisky. He rested his head against the back of the leather chaise and closed his eyes. He'd drunk at least a half-gallon of water but still felt slightly hungover. He fell asleep and when he woke hours later the television was off and Celeste had covered his body with a velvety throw.

She sat on a matching love seat, her sock-covered feet resting on a leather ottoman. She was typing on a laptop while Scamp lay on a towel beside her. He shifted and her head popped up.

"Did you sleep well?"

Moaning softly, Ross stretched his arms above his head. "Yes."

She smiled. "In case you're wondering about the throw, it's mine. I bring it with me whenever I travel because sometimes it gets too cold during a flight, and I don't like using the blankets the airlines provide because I don't know who's used them before me."

Ross brought it to his nose and sniffed it, recognizing the lingering scent as Celeste's perfume. "What are you working on?"

"I'm just typing up a few notes about what I want to write about Bronco. I've confirmed video interviews with you and Brynn, to highlight the men's and women's view of the rodeo, but I'd also like to write at least one more piece and submit it to the station before I leave."

Before I leave. It had become Celeste's mantra and Ross wanted to tell her to stop saying it, because he was more than aware of the inevitable. That she was going to leave Bronco and subsequently file for divorce. And he had no one to blame but himself because he had been the one to establish the conditions for the game both of them knew would end: marriage, no exchange of money, no sex, and divorce.

When he'd come up with the idea Ross thought it would be foolproof because they both had agreed not to become emotionally involved with each other. That sounded good to Ross because unlike his brothers he'd eschewed falling in love and at this time in his life marriage hadn't been in his life plan.

However, everything changed because of a little slip of a reporter who'd unknowingly changed him. He'd come to enjoy being married and a husband to a woman who'd filled up the space and empty hours he hadn't even been aware of.

After spending weeks on the rodeo circuit, he'd looked forward to coming home to kick back and relax. He would saddle Commander and let the powerful stallion gallop at full speed over the countryside before bringing him back to the stable. Riding, mowing, and occasionally repairing the fencing surrounding his property gave Ross a sense of purpose when he wasn't competing. He loved Bronco and Montana, where he felt more alive than he did anywhere else. The mountains, lakes and rivers teeming with bass, and endless miles of grassland had become an aphrodisiac he never tired of. He'd competed in big cities, but what few knew was that he couldn't wait to get back to Bronco.

"Have you thought of who else you'd like to interview?" he asked Celeste.

Her fingers stopped tapping keys when she gave him a direct stare. "Probably an elected official."

"Why an elected official?"

"Because they can talk about occurrences without personalizing. It would be more about policy than their personal accomplishments."

"Have you ever met a politician that didn't blow his or her own horn when it comes to taking credit for something they actually did not do?"

Celeste smiled. "I'm aware of a few, but that's what makes them a politician. They're able to sway their constituents because they possess the skill to tell them what they want to hear."

"You sound a little cynical when it comes to politicians."

"What I don't do, Ross, is believe every word that comes out of their mouths. There was a time when I referred to their tactics as politricks, and I do in-depth research into a politician's background before I decide to give them my vote."

"I find politics messy," Ross admitted.

"Do you vote?"

He nodded. "Yes, but like you I have to believe the candidate is worth my support."

Celeste powered down her laptop and closed it. "You have the personality to become a popular candidate if you decide to run for office."

"I don't think so, Celeste. There are folks who still believe I use women."

"But aren't we working to change that, Ross? There has been a complete one-eighty when it comes to comments on your social media platforms since Nikki's piece aired. Some people attacked the more salacious comments, saying the women were jealous and spiteful and called you a dog because they didn't know you were in love with someone else."

"Still… Thanks, but no thanks, bae. I'll stick to the rodeo and my after-school project."

"Do you feel up to talking about the rodeo today or do you want to wait for another day?" Celeste asked.

"Let's wait a few days because I need to pull out some of the programs and photos from when we first began competing professionally."

"I'm going to put the chicken in the oven, then I'm going to take Scamp for a walk." The puppy's head popped up at the mention of his name.

Ross wanted to ask if she wanted company, but changed his mind because if she'd wanted him to accompany her, he knew Celeste would've mentioned it. She wasn't reticent when it came to speaking her mind.

"Do you want me to check on the chicken while you're out?"

"No. I'm going to set the thermostat low enough for it to cook slowly without burning."

"Is there anything you want me to do for you?"

Smiling, Celeste came to her feet. "Yes. Go upstairs and get into bed and sleep it off. I'll get you up later when it's time to eat."

Ross stood up. "You sound like a nagging wife."

"That's because I am your wife, Ross. And wives are supposed to look after their hardheaded husbands when they do something foolish like drink too much."

"I suppose you're not going to let me live that down."

"I will if you promise never to do it again."

Ross held up a hand. "I promise never to do shots again."

She smiled. "And I promise never to tell anyone that you got so pissy-eyed drunk that you fell face-first on the bed."

"I did?"

"Yes, you did. And I almost threw my back out trying to get you to roll over so I could undress you."

He wiggled his fingers at her. "I'm still offering to give you a massage."

"That's okay. A leisurely soak in a warm bath will suffice."

Ross wiggled his fingers. "But there's magic in these hands."

"Save the magic for when you have to hold on to a rope for eight seconds to beat the buzzer."

"Hey now. Somebody's been studying up on the rodeo."

Celeste rolled her eyes at him. "That's not funny."

He turned serious. "I know you're a city girl, but I told you I'm willing to teach you what you need to know before you submit your piece to the network."

"I'm going to need you to look it over for me before I submit it because I don't want to misquote you."

Ross knew it was time for Celeste to begin working on her interview with him because she didn't want her boss harassing her again. It was obvious the man was determined to increase the station's ratings. And while he'd used his clout to banish Celeste from the newsroom when he'd sent her to Montana to get a story on a subject she knew nothing about, his plan had backfired because her marriage to a rodeo star had become big entertainment news. However, it wasn't enough for Dean Johnson, because now he wanted an interview with her husband within the week. And after she submitted that, Ross wondered what else Dean would want from her.

"I'll read it, and make certain you get all the facts right," Ross reassured her. "How much time do you plan to spend on research before you begin writing?"

"No more than a day. I hope we'll be able to get everything done mid-week, because I need a couple of days to interview Brynn and write up her piece."

Ross smothered a groan when he recalled Brynn inviting him and Celeste to spend the night at the Flying A. And that meant he was expected to share a bed with his wife. The next time would be different because he would be alert, sober, and fully aware of everything.

At that moment Ross wondered how many more times he would be tested when it came to sleeping with Celeste before the time came for her to leave Bronco. He prayed it would only occur twice, because he didn't trust himself if it were to happen a third time.

"Don't worry, Celeste, you'll get it done."

"I have to get it done, Ross, or I'll probably be out of a job."

"I doubt that. Your boss should be happy that you've helped boost the ratings. And he's asked for another story."

"I still have a target on my back when it comes to Dean Johnson. I could give him Emmy award-winning pieces and he'd still want more."

"Have you thought that maybe he likes you? I mean the kind of liking that goes beyond friendship."

Celeste made a sucking sound with her tongue and teeth. "He can like all he wants, but I don't want him. Never did. Never will." She never believed her colleague's story about Dean wanting to date her.

"Do you want your husband to go to Chicago and pay him a visit?"

"Now you're taking this husband-wife thing too far. There's no need for you to go all Neanderthal and confront my boss."

"I won't hit the man, Celeste."

"I don't want you to hit, talk to, or even breathe on him. I took this assignment because I know he wanted me to fail so he could demote me or drum up some false reason to fire me, which he'd have to do since I'm under contract with the network. I couldn't interview Geoff because he wasn't available, and even if I hadn't met you, I still would've come up with a story, even if it meant going to Colorado Springs to talk to some someone at the Professional Rodeo Cowboys Association."

Ross was surprised by this disclosure. "So, you have done your homework?"

"Yes, because I always have to be one step ahead of Dean."

"Well, I'm glad we met because being one step ahead of Dean means I'm enjoying being your husband." The statement reverberated in his head, and he realized he'd said "being" rather than "playing" her husband.

Celeste smiled at him. "It's the same with me. I like that I'm Mrs. Ross Burris."

Ross knew they liked each other, but he also knew their time together would be over in three weeks. And if he were honest with himself, he'd admit he didn't want it to end. He was more than willing to see if they could make it work, and if not, then he would look back and say it was fun while it lasted.

He watched Celeste and Scamp walk out of the family room before he went upstairs. He knew he would miss Celeste when it came time for her to leave. He would miss her mysterious smiles, the sound of her beautifully modulated voice, the lingering scent of her perfume, and the soft sweetness of her mouth whenever he kissed her. She had become more than a wife in name only when she'd taken charge to see that he got home safely the night before. He still did not remember asking her to stay with him. But if he had uttered the words, then Ross knew they had come from his heart, and he realized he had to be careful. Careful that he wasn't falling in love with his wife.

That would spoil everything.

Chapter Eleven

I really like Bronco, but I wonder if I could get used to living here.

There was something about the small town that Celeste had felt drawn to. Everything and everybody seemed to move at a leisurely pace. There were no motorists cutting one another off for a parking space or annoying horn honking or cursing from drivers engaged in escalating road rage.

Strolling along Commercial Street in downtown Bronco Valley, she felt totally relaxed after spending Sunday with Ross because it was the first time since they'd returned from Vegas that they had the entire day to themselves. After dinner, they had gone into the family room to watch a movie both had seen but enjoyed before. Ross lit the fireplace to offset the chill from the dropping temperatures as they cuddled under a blanket while sitting on the sofa. Scamp had whined incessantly until Ross finally picked him up and he scooted under the blanket and fell asleep.

Everything about being married and living with Ross was perfect except when it came time to go to bed. After making certain Scamp was settled for the night, they'd climb the staircase together and then go into their respective bedrooms. Ross would leave his door open as a silent invitation for her to come in if she chose, while Celeste had opted to keep hers closed. It acted as a barrier against temptation, not for Ross but for her.

There were occasions when she suspected he knew that she wanted to make love with him, but then realized it was her own fantasies that had her imagination going into overdrive.

She walked down the street and found Cimarron Rose, the boutique Ross had mentioned where she would find clothes she would like. Celeste peered into the window at the mannequins modeling jeans, tops, and dresses that appealed to her taste.

She entered the shop and noticed several customers staring at her. She knew she was a stranger, but not to the point where she'd become an object of suspicion. Her fears were unfounded when a slender woman with long black hair and stunning green eyes approached her.

"Wait till I tell everyone that one half of the Resties just walked into my shop."

Celeste blinked, then gave the woman a wide-eyed look. "Say what?"

"Aren't you Celeste Burris?"

She nodded. "Yes."

"I'm Everlee, the owner of Cimarron Rose, but everyone calls me Evy. Photos of you and Ross together are all over social media and they're calling you Resties. You know, combining your names, like Bennifer for Ben Affleck and Jennifer Lopez."

Celeste didn't realize marrying Ross had turned them into media darlings. "I'll be certain to let Ross know that."

"Ross and his brothers are already heroes to us in Bronco, but his marrying someone in television really elevates his popularity."

She wanted to tell the pretty young woman that it had been their intent when their Vegas wedding was deliberately leaked to the media. "Ross is pretty special to me."

"I should say he is judging from your incredibly beautiful wedding photos, and I love that you gave a shout-out to the businesses here in Bronco."

"That was intentional," Celeste admitted. She looked around the shop. "I'm here because I need help in choosing something that's different from what I normally wear for work. I need jeans, tops, and maybe a few boho dresses and accessories."

Everlee smiled. "Well, you've come to the right place. I'm certain you'll find everything on your wish list."

Celeste ignored those filming her with their cell phones as she searched through the racks. She had unknowingly become a celebrity in Bronco because she was married to a man who was recognizable in and out of the rodeo arena, and now she was drawn into his sphere even further because the former Celeste Montgomery, sports reporter for a Chicago affiliate, had been labeled a Restie. The portmanteau was catchy, and she was willing to bet Nikki Harper had come up with it.

Ninety minutes later she walked out of Cimarron Rose with four shopping bags. She stored her purchases in the cargo area of the SUV, then headed to a store that sold leather goods to look for boots. The response was identical to the one she'd encountered in the boutique as people welcomed her to Bronco and wished her many happy returns on the marriage to Ross. She bought two pairs of boots and a wide flat-brimmed tan Western hat. If she had married a cowboy, then it was incumbent on her to look the part. Next, she found the flower shop and spent about fifteen minutes there as she purchased several potted plants.

Celeste hadn't realized how exhausting shopping was until she got back to where she had parked. She debated whether to drive over to Bronco Heights and order pizza from Bronco Brick Oven Pizza or stop at Pastabilities because she was craving Italian food. But as she sat behind the wheel she decided to go home and heat up leftovers.

She was pulling into the driveway as Ross was getting out

of his pickup. He waved and walked over to her vehicle as she opened the door to get out.

Ross kissed her forehead. "How was shopping?"

"Exhausting."

"What did you buy?"

"Everything I need so I won't look like a big-city girl. The bags are on the back seats and in the cargo area."

Ross opened the rear door and froze. "Well, damn!" he whispered. "What didn't you buy?"

Celeste smiled. "Underwear. I have more than enough of them."

Ross reached for the shopping bags. "Have you eaten lunch?"

"No. I came home to heat up leftovers."

"Forget about that, Celeste. After we take everything inside, we're going out for lunch. What do you feel like eating?"

"I was thinking about Italian, but I'm so famished right now that I'm willing to eat anywhere."

"We can go to the Gemstone Diner. We don't have to wait long to be served and the food is pretty good."

"Then let's go before my stomach starts making embarrassing noises."

"That's because you hardly touched your breakfast this morning," Ross said, as he reached for another shopping bag.

"That's because I felt queasy."

"Morning sickness?" he teased, wiggling his eyebrows.

"That's not funny, Ross. You know right well that I'm not pregnant."

"No, I don't," he said over his shoulder as he walked to the front door, "but only time will tell because you may have taken advantage of me while I was under the influence."

"What are you now? A stand-up comic? If I wanted to have sex with you, then you'd have to be a willing participant."

Ross stopped suddenly, and Celeste plowed into his back.

"Is that what you want, Celeste? Have you changed your mind about us having sex?"

"No," she lied smoothly.

He turned to stare at her. "You don't sound that convincing."

"I'm sorry if I don't, but I intend to keep to our deal."

Ross walked into the Gemstone Diner with Celeste and found a booth near a window that looked out on the parking lot. Something had altered between them when he'd asked her if she had changed her mind about them having sex. Even though she'd said no, he did not believe her.

There hadn't been many things in his life that Ross wanted, but one of those things was Celeste Burris. And if she'd asked him the same question, he knew he wouldn't be able to lie to her. He wanted nothing more than to take his wife to bed and make endless love to her. However, he knew that wasn't possible.

He recognized familiar voices and looked over to the opposite booth to see Winona Cobbs with her fiancé, Stanley Sanchez. Despite the fact that they were both elderly—Winona was in her nineties, and Stanley was in his late eighties—it was obvious Stanley was angry and accusing Winona of flirting with a younger man.

"How could you disrespect me like that?" Stanley said between clenched teeth. Clearly the man struggled not to raise his voice.

Winona, dressed in her ubiquitous purple that contrasted with her white hair, glared at Stanley. "You're being ridiculous, Stanley. What was I supposed to do? Tell Smitty to stop flirting with me?"

"But you did nothing to discourage him, Winona."

"You must know I have no interest in Smitty or any other man."

Stanley slumped back in the booth and gave his fiancée a

wary look as if he did not believe her. He signaled the wait-ress for the check, then helped Winona up and escorted her out of the diner.

"What was that all about?" Celeste asked Ross once the couple was out of earshot.

He'd felt guilty about eavesdropping on the couple's con-versation, but they had been talking loud enough for several diners to overhear them. "There's much too much drama in committed relationships."

"I agree," she said. "What we have is perfect for me be-cause I know exactly what to expect. And once we break up there will be no animosity or hard feelings."

"It's a little more complicated with Winona and Stanley."

"It can't be because of their ages, Ross. Because love is love regardless of one's age."

Ross waited until they'd given the waitress their order and then said, "Winona happens to be Bronco's resident psychic." Despite Celeste's raised brows, he continued. "She hasn't had it easy. Back in the day, she and Josiah Abernathy were se-cretly young lovers. She was institutionalized after she dis-covered she was pregnant and then was told that her baby was stillborn, but the Abernathys knew the baby was alive, and to avoid a scandal they placed the baby up for adoption. They all left Rust Creek Falls and moved to Bronco."

"Oh, how awful. Are you talking about the same Abernathy family that Brynn is marrying into?"

"Don't look so shocked, bae. It happens every day when families decide to do underhanded things to hide what they consider their dirty linen. Josiah eventually married and had several children, but as he got older and was diagnosed with dementia, he couldn't tell anyone where his daughter was, even though he knew she was still alive."

"Did they ever find her?"

"Yes. Josiah's great-grandson and his fiancée finally found

her. Beatrix, who'd been named Dorothea and nicknamed Daisy, was finally reunited with her birth mother after Winona moved to Bronco. Winona now lives with Daisy."

"So, it ended happily ever after."

"For Winona it did." He took a sip of the water the waitress had brought to the table.

"What about Stanley?" Celeste asked, obviously interested in the couple's story.

"Stanley lost his wife after sixty years of marriage and when he met Winona, he fell instantly in love and asked her to marry him. She agreed but kept putting off setting a date. Word around town is that even though they chose a date, Stanley believes Winona really doesn't want to get married."

"How old are they, Ross?"

"Stanley is in his eighties. Winona…" Ross thought for a second, then shook his head. "Gotta be in her nineties."

"That's so sweet. But how old is the younger man Stanley accuses Winona of flirting with?"

"Smitty's in his early eighties."

Celeste's jaw dropped. "No!" she said, laughing.

"Yes," Ross confirmed. "That goes to show you that jealousy has no age limit. My dad is still jealous of men who try and hit on my mother. Has it happened to you, Celeste?"

She frowned as she studied the printed paper placemat. "Too many times. I'd go out after work with some of my girlfriends for happy hour, and even when we ignored the cheesy pickup lines some men refused to give up until we were forced to insult them."

"What do you say to them?"

Celeste stared at something over his shoulder. "No comment."

Ross crossed his arms over his chest. "Are you saying that you dropped a few f-bombs."

"I said no comment, Ross."

"Of course, you did," he said, grinning. "So, my wife can go a couple of rounds with the best of them."

"Your wife can hold her own when it comes to deflecting the advances of men who don't know when to quit bugging the hell out of her."

"I doubt if you'll have that problem here in Bronco because every man in town knows you're Celeste Burris."

"Are you aware that people are calling us Resties?"

He hadn't heard the term himself and asked Celeste to explain it. "You don't sound thrilled, but isn't that what you predicted when we went public with our marriage? It looks as if you got your wish."

Celeste counted slowly to five so as not to lose her temper. "It wasn't what I'd wished for, Ross. It was just a statement of fact."

"And as a journalist you only deal in facts."

"Yes," she said. "And the fact is our marriage isn't going to extend beyond May," she continued in a hushed whisper.

Ross lowered his arms, resting his elbows on the table. "I don't want to talk about that. Not now and not here."

Celeste refused to back down or wither under his angry glare. "We're going to have to talk about it at some time."

"I'm aware of that, but just not now." His brown eyes scanned the half-full diner.

She wanted to tell him that he was in denial because whenever she mentioned going back to Chicago it was as if she were talking to herself. He'd responded like a bell without a clapper.

"Okay. Not here, but it's something we must talk about."

"You talk about it all the time whenever you mention going back to Chicago."

"That's a given, Ross, because even Stephanie asked during our Zoom call about my working in Chicago while you'll be living here in Bronco. It was the same with Nikki during our interview. People are aware that I'll be leaving Bronco to go back to Chicago, so that shouldn't raise alarms bells when they no longer see us together."

"I know but there's no need for you to keep bringing it up."

"If it bothers you I—"

"It does bother me." Ross interrupted her. "I don't like to be nagged about something I'm more than well aware of."

She sat back, her spine hitting the cushion of the booth. "Do you realize that this is the second time you've referred to me as a nag?"

"I didn't mean it," he said quickly.

"Yes, you did, Ross, or you wouldn't have said it."

A beat passed, then he said, "Do you realize we're having our first fight as a married couple?"

Reaching across the table, Celeste rested her hand on his. "We're not fighting. What we have is a failure to communicate."

"You're going 'Cool Hand Luke' on me?"

"Yes, I am, cowboy."

The lines of tension bracketing Ross's mouth eased. "You like calling me that, don't you?"

"You are a cowboy, Ross. Even the organization is called the Professional Rodeo Cowboys Association."

"I'll own it because Bill Picket was not only Black, but was one of the first great rodeo cowboys, at a time when white rodeo riders were called cowhands. For that reason he is honored to be called a cowboy. He was finally inducted into the ProRodeo Hall of Fame in 1989. The Burrises compete every year in the Bill Pickett Invitational Rodeo that celebrates Black cowboys and cowgirls in the history of the American west. The events sell out every year."

"Now, that that's something I would like to attend."

Ross studied Celeste thoughtfully for a moment. "That can be arranged if we're still in touch with each other."

"There's no reason why we would have to lose touch. I'd attend as a reporter covering a sporting event."

Although Ross had mentioned keeping in touch with Celeste, he wondered if he'd spoken too soon. Once they were divorced it would be detrimental to his emotional well-being to be around his ex-wife. And what if she became involved with someone and… His thoughts trailed off because he did not want to think of Celeste with another man.

The waitress set their selections on the table and Ross realized the woman had given him Celeste's spaghetti and meatballs and Celeste his broiled sole and yellow rice. He waited until she walked away before switching plates.

After unfolding a napkin, Celeste spread it over her lap. "This smells good."

"It is good," Ross said. "I've ordered it a few times." Her cell phone chimed a ringtone, the one he recognized as her boss's. Celeste ignored it. "Aren't you going to answer that?"

"Nope. Whatever Dean wants to tell me can wait until I finish eating."

Celeste had tired of being at Dean's every beck and call. She'd compromised her integrity to boost the station's ratings and had promised to file more stories over the coming weeks, so it was time for him to ease up and give her some space.

"Good for you."

"Why would you say that?" she asked after chewing and swallowing a piece of perfectly seasoned meatball.

"You've given him what he needs to boost ratings, so don't you think it's time he should stop pressuring you to do more."

"He can't do that because the man's a narcissist. It's always all about him."

"The next time he contacts you, do you want me to answer the call?"

"And say what, Ross? That if he doesn't stop harassing your wife, you're going to knock him on his ass?"

Grinning, Ross kissed his muscled biceps. "I know he wouldn't mess with these guns."

"Showoff. Put your arms down," Celeste whispered when a woman sitting at a table several feet away stared at him. "You're embarrassing me."

Ross winked at her. "Sorry about that, love."

She knew he was putting on an act for the benefit of others. Ross never broke character, while she had continued to struggle in her attempt to make everyone believe she was in love with her husband. The endearments did not come as easily for her as they did for Ross, but she hoped that with time she, too, would be able to give an award-winning performance until it came time for her to leave Bronco.

Celeste began the task of emptying the bags with her purchases and removing price tags as soon as they arrived back at the house. "I think I overdid it," she said when Ross walked into the family room.

He sank down to the floor beside her. "You think? How many pairs of jeans did you buy?"

"Six. If I'm going to ride horses, then I'm going to need a pair for every day of the week."

Ross picked up an off-the-shoulder floral print tube peasant shirt. "This is very pretty. And so is this one," he added as he held up a white ruffle trim–layered blouse.

"I decided to buy a few nice blouses to wear with jeans to jazz up the outfit."

"Do you have an outfit that you can wear to a fancy restaurant?"

"What do you have in mind? 'Little black dress' kind of fancy?"

"I'd like to take you to a restaurant that has amazing views of the entire city. It's very, very high-end, and only has two seatings each night."

"That does sound fancy."

"Should I make reservations for our Saturday date night?"

Celeste agreed because aside from going to Doug's with Ross it had been a long time since she'd had a date night. Once she'd broken up with DeAndre, she spent her weekends at home listening to music or watching movies on various streaming services.

"Are we going to have date night every Saturday?" she asked, when Ross took his cell phone off a side table.

"Yes. Remember, we must make it look good for everyone to believe that we're crazy in love."

"Oh, now you're going Beyoncé on me," she teased.

He laughed. "How about this one? 'Do you understand the words coming out of my mouth?'"

"*Rush Hour*," Celeste said. "Let me know if you recognize this one. 'Here's your bobby pin, here's your bobby pin, and here's your punk-ass bobby pin.'"

"That's too easy, bae. *Tower Heist*."

"You're just full of surprises, Ross. I never would've figured you would be into movie trivia."

Ross smiled and said, "There's a lot of things you'll discover about me now that we're living together."

Celeste knew he was right as she continued unpacking bags and boxes while he called to make dinner reservations for Saturday. When Dean had assigned her to interview Geoff Burris, not only hadn't she known anything about the sport, but she was unfamiliar with the personality of a rodeo performer.

It was different with baseball, football, and basketball players because many of them attended and were recruited from colleges. When Ross mentioned that his brother Mike was in medical school, she'd recalled interviewing a football player who'd attended med school in the off season to become a trauma surgeon. Celeste did not view professional athletes as having all brawn and no brains because many were highly intelligent and had gone on to other professions and ventures after retiring from the game.

What she did discover about Ross Burris was there was more to him than his gorgeous face and body. Yes, he was charming and personable, which added to his overall magnetic personality. That was what he'd projected as a rodeo rider to the delight of his many fans. But behind closed doors Celeste had discovered the more serious Ross who wanted to establish an after-school program for Bronco's youth. A safe place where students could gather for extra help, free of charge, with their homework and tutoring for test prep.

Celeste hadn't wanted to believe the negative comments about him on social media because she was of the mindset that there were always two sides to every story, and she'd discovered the real-life Ross Burris was nothing like the one being trolled on social media.

Ross claimed he could deal with the negative comments because he knew they weren't true; however, he was more concerned about how they'd affected his family. The Burris name was held in high regard in rodeo, and he did not want it besmirched with scathing comments about his treatment of women.

She wasn't certain whether the people in Bronco chose to ignore the less than favorable comments about Ross, but to them he was their hometown hero and that spoke volumes. They knew and respected him and his family.

Ross ended his call. "We have a reservation for seven at Coeur de l'Ouest."

"Oo la la. *Ça a l'air très français et chic.*"

He stared at her for several seconds, then burst into laughter. "It sounded beautiful, but I didn't understand a word you said."

"I said it sounds very French and fancy," Celeste translated.

"It is. Do you speak fluent French?"

"*Oui, monsieur.* I took it in high school and in college, but I perfected it when I had a college roommate who was from Montreal and would speak to me exclusively in French. I don't get the chance to speak it much now, but I will watch French-speaking movies to keep fluent."

"Is that the reason you want to travel to Europe? So, you can speak French?"

"That's not the only reason. What I want is to experience other cultures. I want to stay in hostels and soak up some of the history, experiment eating different dishes, and see the countries through the eyes of the locals, while avoiding what I'd call the tourists traps."

"Have you ever traveled abroad?" Ross asked her.

"No. I've been to many Caribbean islands on vacation, but never overseas. Have you?"

Ross hadn't traveled out of the States, except when he'd participated in the Calgary Stampede in Alberta, Canada, and he was looking forward to when he would be able to travel for an extended period. "No, but I am looking forward to it one of these days. I'm happy Geoff and Stephanie took the opportunity."

"It will happen for you, Ross, once your nonprofit is up and running."

"You're right, but that isn't going to be for a while. I've secured a loan to cover the renovations on the building, but I still have a lot to do. My mother and father have agreed to help, but I'm looking forward to signing on more volunteers."

"How many more, Ross?"

"I won't know until we determine how many kids will sign up."

Celeste noticed he'd said *we* as if she was included in the equation. And she knew if the circumstances were different and she'd opted to stay in Bronco, then she would've signed on to volunteer or mentor a student interested in a career in journalism. He'd shared the prospectus with her, and she was confident his project would be successful.

She removed the Stetson from the hat box and put it on. "How do I look?"

Ross scooted closer and kissed her cheek. "Beautiful. Now you're a real cowgirl."

Her smile was dazzling. "There's no way I'm going to allow my man to outshine me when we're out and about together."

"Don't even go there, Celeste. You're so beautiful I have to step up my game to keep up with you. I don't think you know how many dudes were gawking at you when we walked into Doug's, and while I was waiting at the bar with Garrett, I overheard a few of them refer to you as a Carolina reaper."

Celeste's jaw dropped and it was several seconds before she said, "They likened me to the hottest pepper on the planet?"

"What can I say, sweetheart? You're hot!" She waved off his effusive words and he asked her, "You don't agree? How do you see yourself, Celeste?"

A slight frown appeared between her eyes. "See myself how?"

"As a woman."

Celeste pondered Ross's question, and recalled it was the same thing her father had asked her once she'd made the decision to become a broadcast reporter. Was she ready to face the opposition some women endured when they'd asked for a seat at the table that had been exclusive for men?

"When it comes to my career, I'm a journalist who just happens to be a woman. I refuse to be pigeonholed and put in the box labeled 'female sports reporter.' I've paid my dues, earned my graduate degree in journalism, and I refuse to let anyone define me as a journalist or as a woman.

"I've had men call me names I refuse to repeat, and some even bold enough to tell me what they'd like to do with me, but it never deterred me from completing my assignment. Dean isn't much different from those men. He's just more subtle. I know for a fact that he didn't want me as the backup sports reporter and was told by the head of the network that he had to accept me because they wanted more diversity and inclusion. And I know if I'd been a man, our working relationship would be a lot different. But Dean has underestimated me, because when and if I do leave WWCH it will be on my terms and not because he forced me out."

"If you were to go to another network, would it be in Chicago or another large city?"

"Probably, Ross, because I'm a big-city girl. I like Bronco, but I'm used to twenty-four-hour delis, high-fashion shops, and luxury hotels along the Magnificent Mile, museum exhibits, and professional sports teams."

"Why do I get the impression that you think of Bronco as boring?"

"Not boring, Ross. It has a laid-back vibe that, given time, I could get used to. What I wouldn't miss about living in a big city is the noise from car horns and sirens."

Ross nodded. "I really appreciate Bronco whenever I take a break from competing."

"How often is that?"

"A lot more often now than in the past. I'm scheduled to join the circuit the second week in June, but I'll be back for the Bronco Summer Family Rodeo."

Celeste recalled Audrey talking about the event and assumed it was a big deal, like the Kentucky Derby or the Indianapolis 500. "I'm sorry I won't get to see you compete."

"So am I."

She wasn't certain, but was there regret in those three words?

She hoped he wasn't sending her conflicting messages. They'd agreed to a termination date for their marriage. Once it came, she would leave Bronco and her husband behind, to resume the life she had in Chicago.

Chapter Twelve

Celeste's plan to interview Ross hit a slight speed bump when he informed her that he had to drive Jeremy to Billings and planned to wait there to see if the doctors at the VA hospital wanted to keep him overnight for a battery of tests.

Now that she had extra time on her hands, she decided to drive into town and talk to some of the local elected officials. Including them in some of the pieces for the network would add interesting facts about the city. At the Bronco city hall, she gave the woman at the reception desk her name, but it was apparent the woman knew who she was when she congratulated her on her recent marriage to one of their own.

"Thank you. I'm a reporter with a Chicago television station and I'd like to talk to Mayor Smith. I'm doing a piece on Bronco residents, and I would like to include the mayor's comments."

The elderly woman smiled. "The mayor has an open-door policy, so you just march right in and tell him what you want."

Celeste thanked her again and walked down a hall to the mayor's office. How different it was for her to gain access to a politician in Chicago. First, she had to formally request an interview, then wait until her credentials were checked and validated before she was given an appointment, days and sometimes weeks down the road. The senior sportswriter at the network said he had to wait more than two weeks to interview city officials after the Cubs won the World Series in 2016.

Mayor Rafferty Smith stood up as she walked in and introduced herself.

"I know exactly who you are because the entire town has been buzzing about Ross Burris eloping with a television reporter. Everyone was shocked. We had no idea he was dating someone." He pulled out a chair at a small round table. "Please sit down. I always feel more comfortable not sitting behind the desk talking to folks."

"Thank you." Celeste took an immediate liking to the man who didn't like standing on ceremony.

The mayor folded his hands on the top of the table. "Now, tell me, what brings you here today?"

"I'm doing a piece on the rodeo and plan to interview Ross Burris and Brynn Hawkins."

"Well, what is you want to ask me?"

She took out a handheld tape recorder and placed it on the table, then removed a small spiral notebook with a list of questions she'd planned to ask the man. "I'd like to know about Bronco and why people want to live and work here."

"That's an easy question to answer."

The interview lasted fifteen minutes with the mayor telling her about the history of Bronco and how the population grew exponentially with the influx of new residents looking for a slower pace and better quality of life. He liked that Bronco was racially and ethnically diverse and regardless of their economic status, everyone in Bronco supported one another. He'd mentioned the weeklong Fourth of July celebration, featuring something for everyone, and the Mistletoe Rodeo that brought folks in from all over Montana and nearby states.

"I'm new to Bronco, but is there any truth to the rumor about your wife's necklace having special powers?"

"Do you intend to include this in your piece?"

"Oh no," Celeste said, as she turned off the tape recorder. "This is definitely off the record."

"I'd given my wife, Penny, a pearl necklace for our thirtieth wedding anniversary, but somehow it disappeared during the party, and no one knew what had happened to it. The necklace wound up in a vintage shop, but someone recognized that it belonged to Penny, and I just got it back this morning. There's a rumor that it brings good luck to those who touch the pearls. Would you like to see the necklace?"

"Yes, I would." Celeste loved pearls. She had her own strand that she'd inherited from her grandmother.

The mayor went to his desk and unlocked a drawer. He returned to the table with a flat box and handed it to Celeste. "Open it and tell me what you think."

She opened the box to find a strand of perfectly matched pearls. "They are beautiful."

Mayor Smith puffed out his chest. "They are, if I may say so myself. You can touch them if you'd like, but you probably don't need the luck because you've already married the man you love."

Celeste ran her fingertips over the smooth pearls. "You're right about my not needing luck." Marrying Ross had saved her career.

"You can try it on."

"Are you sure?"

"Very sure. Penny doesn't know it, but I plan to give it to her when I get home tonight."

Celeste removed the necklace from the case and fastened the strand around her neck. Even though the pearls felt cool against her throat, it wasn't the same with her face. It was on fire.

"They look so nice on you, Celeste. I know my Penny is going be over the moon once she discovers I'd found the necklace."

Reaching up, Celeste released the clasp and put the necklace back in its case. Maybe her feeling different did have something to do with the pearl necklace. Perhaps it did have special powers. However, she wasn't superstitious by nature, but then anything was possible.

She stood up. "Thank you for your time, Mayor. I'll send you a copy of the piece before I submit it for your approval."

"I really appreciate that." He paused. "Have you thought about writing for the *Bronco Bulletin*?"

Celeste shook her head. "I won't be able to write for the local paper because of an exclusivity clause in my contract."

"When does your contract expire?"

"The end of June."

"That's not too far off. Do you intend to re-sign with the same clause?"

The mayor was asking Celeste questions to which she did not have an answer. "I don't know. I haven't thought about it." Dean hadn't mentioned renewing her contract, but that was before her marriage to Ross had boosted ratings. She would have to wait until she returned to Chicago to discuss it with HR. And if she did renew, then it would be based on a promotion and an increase in salary.

"Don't think too long because we need a reporter with your experience here in Bronco. And there's also the TV station in Billings that I'm certain would hire you."

Celeste wanted to tell the mayor that he was getting ahead of himself, but couldn't because he didn't know once she left Bronco she did not plan to come back.

She thanked him for his time and drove home to type up her notes while they were still fresh in her mind. Mayor Smith had answered all her questions, but he'd also raised some interesting ones for her.

Celeste didn't know why as she walked inside the house, but she felt different. And the difference was her feelings for Ross were intensifying with each passing day. Not only was she in denial but she had lied to herself and to Ross that she didn't want them to sleep together. They were newlyweds, husband and wife, and other than what she now deemed an asinine agreement between them they should have consummated their marriage.

Ross returned home late that afternoon to find Celeste on the sofa in the family room, laptop resting on her knees and an earpiece in one ear. It wasn't until he saw the tape recorder on the cushion beside her that he realized she was transcribing her notes. Her head popped up when he attempted to back out of the room because he didn't want to disturb her. She removed the earpiece and shut off the recorder.

"Please don't leave, Ross."

He walked in and sat next to her. There was something so alluring and sensual about her that he found it difficult to draw a normal breath. She'd haphazardly styled her hair in a loose ponytail but instead of appearing disheveled, in his mind she looked like he'd made love to her.

"How was your day?"

She closed the laptop and set it on the floor. "I'll let you know after you kiss me."

Ross was shocked that she'd asked him to kiss her, when in the past it was always him making the request. "Is that what you really want?" he whispered in her ear.

"Of course. "Don't husbands kiss their wives when they come home?" she asked teasingly.

Shifting slightly, he wrapped his arms around her waist and eased her forward until she lay between his outstretched legs. Celeste wanted him to kiss her when he just wanted to feel her against him. He lowered his head and buried his face in her coconut-scented hair. She looked and smelled good enough to eat. And that's what he wanted to do. Taste every inch of her silken skin.

Ross felt the rapid beating of her heart against his chest as she buried her face against his neck. "Are you okay?"

"Yes." The single word was a soft sigh.

He smiled. Celeste might be okay, but he was on fire. His hands were busy easing up the hem of her blouse so they could explore the hollow of her back. His hands became bolder when they slipped under the waistband of her jeans to cup her hips. He wished they could stay like this forever.

Celeste raised her head and met his eyes before she kissed him with a hunger that had been building for days. She'd become sleep deprived because of the erotic dreams that had kept her from a peaceful night's rest. And she was glad that Ross's bedroom was across the hall, and her door was closed, because he couldn't hear her moaning whenever her body betrayed her. Long-forgotten orgasms were back, attacking her relentlessly, and she was forced to press her face into the pillows to muffle her screams.

Celeste wasn't certain why she'd asked Ross to kiss her but realized she had been fighting her attraction to him within minutes of meeting him at DJ's Deluxe. It just wasn't his good looks. It was how she felt whenever he looked at her. It was as if he could see behind her facade of indifference when she denied wanting to make love with him. Her lips said one thing while her traitorous body said the opposite.

"I missed seeing you this morning," she whispered, as she nibbled on his lower lip.

"But I told you that I had to go to Billings."

"I know."

"If you know, then what is it, Celeste?"

"I like you, Ross. I like you so much more than I should."

She did not have time to react when he reversed their positions, and he lay atop her, supporting most of his weight on his forearms. Celeste smiled as she examined his face, feature by feature, unable to believe that he belonged to her and she to him. She had married Ross, taken his name, and now she wanted him to take her to his bed.

"Why are you telling me this?" Ross asked.

"Because I have to clear my conscience."

He laughed softly. "Liking me too much bothers you?"

"Yes, it does."

"It's normal for married people to like each other."

"But we're not normal married people, Ross. We live together, present as a couple in public, but once we come home and go to our respective bedrooms that's where the normalcy ends." Less than four feet separated their two bedrooms, but it could have been a chasm as wide as the Grand Canyon because of what she now considered an asinine pretext that their marriage would be in name only. She and Ross were consenting adults and she knew if they had met under a different set of circumstances, they would have made love.

Ross rolled off her body and sat up, easing her up with him. "Are saying you want us to sleep together?"

Celeste realized she'd reached the point of no return; she'd opened the door and now she wouldn't be able to close it. Her feelings for Ross had intensified to where the liking had shifted to loving. She had fallen for her husband; she didn't want an annulment or a divorce, but knew it wasn't the time to tell him that. And they'd promised each other there would be no sex, and she didn't want to be the first one to break the promise.

"No. I want the pretense to stop," she said instead. "I can't continue pretending that I'm the loving wife in public and your friend whenever we're behind closed doors." The sexual tension was beginning to affect her emotional well-being.

"Do you really think this has been easy on me?" Ross rubbed the back of his neck, his hands fisted. "I'm married to a woman who turns me the hell on, and there's nothing I can do about it."

"Don't blame me, Ross, because you're the one who came up with the rule that we would not have sex."

"Yes, dammit! And you agreed."

"Yes, I did agree because I wanted to save my job and your reputation."

"What is it you want?" Ross asked, after the seconds ticked into a full minute. "Just tell me and I'll do it."

"I want us to stop being lovey-dovey, kissy-face in public. Everyone in Bronco knows we're married, so we don't have to act like a couple of horny teenagers who have to touch each other as if we fear the other will disappear."

Ross nodded. "What else?"

"That's it."

"Okay. I'll pull back with the affection whenever we're out together."

Twin emotions of relief and sadness swept over Celeste, and she felt alone, bereft. She'd asked Ross to stop the public displays of affection because her feelings had changed. Feelings she was helpless to control.

She stood up as tears welled up in her eyes and she blinked at them before they fell. She turned her head, but she wasn't quick enough when Ross stared at her like a deer in the headlights. He appeared rooted to the spot as the tears fell down her cheeks. It had been more than eight years since she'd shed tears and that was at her grandmother's funeral, and now that she was Celeste Burris she'd cried twice in the span of a week.

She turned on her heels and ran out of the family room and up the staircase to her bedroom where she lay across the bed sobbing about making a mess of her life.

When she'd boarded the flight from O'Hare to Billings, it was with the determination that she would succeed. Dean Johnson had banished her from the newsroom to go where she'd never been to interview someone about a sport she'd known absolutely nothing about. She'd spewed a litany of curses as she packed her bags, then vowed no matter what Dean said or did he would not break her.

Fast-forward and she was now the wife of a popular rodeo rider who, along with his brothers, had achieved the status of local heroes. While she'd become a modern-day Cinderella who'd met her prince, fallen in love, married, and would live happily ever after.

However, Celeste's fairy-tale bubble burst when all the lies had become truths. The stories about meeting and falling in love at first sight were real, because Celeste Burris nee Montgomery had found herself in love with her husband.

Ross headed toward the staircase, taking two steps at a time. He didn't know what had happened after he'd left to drive Jeremy to Billings, but he knew Celeste wasn't the same woman he'd left at home.

He'd gotten up earlier than usual to let the horses out, and then returned to the house to shower and change before picking up Jeremy to take him to the VA hospital. He'd waited hours before a nurse informed him Jeremy's doctor wanted to keep him overnight. And when he returned to Bronco it was to a woman he recognized but didn't know. Celeste claiming she'd missed him echoed his own sentiments because he'd missed seeing her when he'd returned to the house that morning and hadn't found her waiting to hand him a mug of steaming coffee. He'd come to cherish those moments together.

She'd admitted his public displays of affection agitated her because once they came home and closed the door they became roommates. In other words, they had to be all in or all out. And she'd made it known to him that she wanted out.

Ross stood at the entrance to the bedroom, staring at the slender figure on the king-size bed he should have shared with her. He walked over to the bed, sat on the side of the mattress, and rested a hand on her back.

"It's okay, baby. I'm willing to go along with whatever you want."

"Stay here with me."

Ross knew Celeste was vulnerable and he didn't want to take advantage of her. "For how long?"

"Until I fall asleep."

He shifted her until she lay in the middle of the bed, then folded his body next to hers. Ross smiled when she turned to her side to face him. He dabbed at the moisture on her cheeks with the pad of his thumb. Ross knew he was in denial because he'd admitted to Celeste that she turned him on, but what he refused to say was that he loved her. That their charade had become a reality that rocked him to his core because Ross Burris had fallen in love for the first time in his life— and with his wife.

He wasn't certain when it had happened, but that no longer mattered. His vow not to become involved, not to cross or blur the lines so when came time for him to drive her to Billings Logan International Airport for her flight back to Chicago it would be accomplished with little or no fanfare. He would wish her safe travels, kiss her goodbye, and walk out of the terminal to close that chapter of his life with his temporary wife.

Ross waited until Celeste fell asleep, then slipped off the bed. She was right about toning them down because it would make it easier for her when it came time for her to leave. And he could not forget why she had come to Bronco.

And it was not to stay.

Celeste and Ross had become roommates and polite strangers behind closed doors, and it was what she'd needed to not only get her emotions in check but also to remind herself why she'd come to Bronco.

For the last several days Ross had gotten up early to care for the horses, while she'd been up, showered, and dressed when he returned to offer him coffee. After breakfast she'd retreated to the family room to work. That morning she'd forwarded the piece with Mayor Smith to Dean for the network's weekend Places and Spaces segment.

She didn't have to wait long for Dean's response. Her cell phone dinged shortly after with his programmed ringtone. "Yes, Dean."

"I like your piece on the mayor. But do you think you can get some more footage of the downtown area and some of the cattle ranches the mayor talked about?"

Celeste shook her head and closed her eyes, grateful that they weren't on FaceTime. "I'll ask Mayor Smith if the photographer for the *Bronco Bulletin* can send you some stills and videos."

"Good. What about the piece on Burris? We want to air it right after the one about the town."

"I'm working on it."

"Why do you always say that?"

"Because it's true." She paused, not wanting to tell her boss what exactly was on her mind. That she was seriously considering going to HR to file a complaint charging him with harassment. "You must stop calling me and interrupting me when I'm working, Dean."

"There's no way I can know if you're working because you're not here in the newsroom."

"Send me a text or email and I'll get back to you whenever I can."

"The clock is ticking, Celeste, and the higher-ups are breathing down my neck to make certain the ratings keep going up, and that's not going to be possible with you dragging your feet getting us this piece on Burris."

"This conversation is over. Good afternoon, Dean," she said, ending the call.

Celeste heard clapping and turned to see Ross standing

several feet away. She hadn't heard him come into the room, and it wasn't the first time that she marveled how a man his size was able to move so quietly.

"I didn't hear what your boss was saying but I bet he didn't like you hanging up on him."

Celeste unfolded her legs and smiled at Ross when he sat opposite her. Things had changed between them after her somewhat emotional meltdown several days ago, and for the better. There hadn't been any PDAs because they hadn't gone out together. When she'd given Ross a list of needed groceries, he'd driven into town to pick them up.

She preferred it when he was away from the house because it had become her time—her time to spend hours on her laptop doing research and her time to think about her future.

"I've had it up to my eyeballs with Dean relentlessly hounding me for more stories." Her phone pinged again. "That's him calling me back."

"Are you going to answer it?" Ross asked.

Celeste shook her head. "No. I don't want to talk to him. If he wants to communicate with me, then it will have to be by text message or email, because if I talk directly to him, then I'm going to say something that will get me fired."

Ross wondered if Celeste's mini meltdown the other day resulted from her ongoing tense relationship with her boss. That she hadn't been able to keep up the ruse that they were in love because she'd felt pressured from both sides: her husband and her boss.

Her revelation that she liked him more than she should went double for him, because what he felt for Celeste went beyond mere liking. He had fallen in love with her. What he still was attempting to process was their compatibility.

She wasn't like some women he'd met who'd clung to him like Velcro. They'd complained that they didn't see him enough and he'd had to remind them he was involved in a sport that kept him away from home for weeks at a time. It was the same with Celeste. Her position as a sports reporter took her away from Chicago. Ross knew if they did decide to stay together then their unorthodox work schedules would keep them apart for extended lengths of time. How would they work it out?

Lassoing his errant thoughts, he focused on Celeste and her boss. "What is he bugging you about now?"

"He wants my interview with you."

"I know you wanted to wait until after you interviewed Brynn, but I'm more than willing to begin now." Brynn had called to say she was available later in the week and they'd made arrangements to go out to the Flying A on Thursday afternoon and stay overnight.

Celeste got up and sat next to him. "We can do it tomorrow. I'll call Rylee at the convention center to see if the videographer is available to tape the interview. Meanwhile, I'm still compiling my list of questions I'd like to ask you, but first I need you to tell me everything about the rodeo. Even though I've spent hours online searching various sites about the sport, I don't feel like I know exactly what it feels like to be a rodeo rider."

"What do you want to know?"

"Everything, Ross, from mutton busting to bull riding."

He chuckled, remembering the first time he sat on the back of a sheep, struggling to hang on long enough to win a prize. "Do you want to tape this, or just take notes?"

"I'll take notes." She pushed to her feet. "I'll be right back."

Ross glanced around the family room as he waited for Celeste to return. She'd been using the space as her office, and whenever he saw her either sitting on an area rug or on the chaise with her laptop, he'd thought about her suggestion that he convert the smaller outbuilding on the property into a home office. It was close enough to the house to get to during inclement weather, and it would offer enough space and privacy to work undisturbed.

She returned with several steno pads and a handful of sharpened pencils and sat opposite him. "Ready."

"I'll speak slowly so you can jot it all down," he said.

"No need. I have my own form of speed writing. My grandmother was an English teacher who also taught typing and shorthand. She won several typing contests because she was able to type 120 words or more a minute."

"Talk about magic fingers," Ross joked.

"Grammy was incredible. She's the reason I wanted to be a journalist. During the summer she would take me on trips to the zoos, museums, and other places of interest, and then ask that I write something about our adventures for her scrapbooks. I had no idea she'd saved my compositions until we cleaned out her house after her passing."

"It sounds as if you were very close to your grandmother."

"We were very close, Ross. I was named for her, and I still feel her spirit whenever I wear her pearl necklace and earrings."

Ross recalled her wearing the jewelry when he'd first met her at DJ's Deluxe. Her tailored pantsuit, designer heels, and handbag screamed big city and made her a standout in Bronco.

Suddenly Ross wanted to know more about the woman he'd married beyond what she'd disclosed about her parents and brothers. "What about your grandfather?"

"Grandpa was a big man with a big belly laugh and my brothers would tickle him just to hear him laugh. I was eight when he was killed after his car was hit head-on by an unlicensed sixteen-year-old drug addict who never should've been behind the wheel. He and my grandmother were high school sweethearts who'd admitted they'd fallen in love at first sight and were married a month after their college graduation. Grammy claimed they could have been real-life protagonists in a romance novel."

"Do you believe in love at first sight, Celeste?"

A hint of a smile, the mysterious smile that had transfixed

him when he saw her headshot for the first time, curved her sexy mouth, and Ross found that he was unable to look away. At the same time he silently berated himself as soon as the question rolled off his tongue. He'd known his feelings for Celeste intensified every day even though he hadn't been willing to act on them, because that would make him the dog he'd been labeled on social media.

"No. I've found myself attracted to some men, but I can honestly say that it wasn't love at first sight. I must be in a relationship to experience that emotion. Why did you ask?"

"I was just curious."

She smiled wider, the expression lighting up her eyes. "You know what they say about curiosity."

"Yeah. It killed the cat, but satisfaction brought it back."

"Speaking of satisfaction," Celeste said, sobering, "I know I won't get to experience that until I get my boss off my back, so we'd better get to work."

"Do you actually think he'll stop, Celeste?"

"Only time will tell."

Chapter Thirteen

Celeste had filled one steno pad with her shorthand symbols when lengthening afternoon shadows prompted her to stop and turn on a table lamp. When Ross described different rodeo events, she'd registered the passion in his voice as he talked about barrel racing, bareback riding, team roping, steer wrestling, bull riding, and tie-down roping. She'd concentrated on jotting down his words rather than intermittently interrupting or glancing over at him.

Everything that made Ross Burris who he was was imprinted on her brain. If he were a suspect in a crime and she a witness, Celeste knew she would be able to give a sketch artist a description of his face that would become an exact image of the flesh and blood man.

There wasn't anything she did not like about him. Aside from his gorgeous face and mischievously laughing eyes, she'd found herself drawn to his deep, silky voice, his speech pattern distinctively Midwest, but with a few words that had a slight Canadian accent. Then there was his strong masculine mouth framed by a neatly barbered mustache and goatee. There weren't enough adjectives to describe his tall, lean, broad-shouldered, naturally muscular body with impressive six-pack abs.

It wasn't only his physical assets that made Ross very attractive, but it was also the way he treated her. There was never a time when he hadn't been the perfect gentleman. Even when they pretended they were hopelessly in love for the benefit of others, his caresses and kisses never bordered on carnal, which would have made her visibly uncomfortable.

"I think I have enough for now," Celeste said, closing the pad. Listing everything she found attractive about Ross suddenly made the room close around her.

Ross pressed the back of his head against the cushion of the butter-soft off-white sofa and stared at the plants on the mahogany coffee table. When Celeste had mentioned making changes in the house, she'd purchased the succulents in painted glazed pots to add a splash of color in what had become his favorite room in the house. The former owners had shipped almost all the furniture in the house overseas to fill their estate and several rooms remained unfurnished. His mother had offered to help him select furniture, but Ross wanted to wait until he quit the rodeo circuit and was no longer traveling.

He stretched. "It's time I see about getting the horses indoors."

"May I go with you?" Celeste asked him.

He gave her a questioning stare. "Really?"

"Yes, really. Why do you look so shocked?"

"Do I?"

"Yeah, you do."

Ross did not want to admit that she had surprised him with the request. He'd taken her to see the small grazing herd the first day she'd come to live with him, and she hadn't seemed at all interested in seeing them again. "Go and put your boots on. I'll be waiting by the truck."

He did not have to wait long. Celeste walked out of the house wearing jeans, a flannel plaid shirt, denim jacket, and blue Doc Martens. With her bare face and ponytail, she could've easily passed for a college student—not a twenty-eight-year-old television reporter.

She was a chameleon morphing from fashionable to casual chic, and now typical cowgirl.

Ross opened the passenger door, waited for her to get in, then rounded the pickup to sit behind the wheel. He'd hoped Celeste asking to accompany him meant she was warming to living in the country, that perhaps she would feel comfortable enough to change her mind about leaving. He wanted to tell her once her contract expired, she could apply for a position with another television affiliate in Billings. While Montana did not have any professional sports teams, high school and college football and basketball were extremely popular.

He'd been tempted to extoll the virtues of living in the Treasure State because of its natural beauty, the Rocky Mountains, an abundance of natural resources and diverse wildlife, but stopped himself because he didn't want to sound like the poster boy for Montana tourism.

"I've discovered that Bronco is beautiful during this time of day," she said.

Ross smiled. It was as if Celeste had read his mind. "Montana is beautiful anytime of the day or year."

Celeste gave him a sidelong glance. "Bragging?"

"Nope. Just stating the facts. There's always something to do here. Winters are perfect for skiing, snowboarding, snowmobiling, dog sledding, and sleigh rides. We have an overabundance of rivers and lakes for boating and fly-fishing, historic caves, and rugged hiking trails. And, of course, we have our share of rodeos and powwows. But the granddaddies of them all are Glacier and Yellowstone National Parks."

"You forgot to mention cattle, bison, bears, wolves, moose, coyotes, bighorn sheep, elk, and mountain lions."

"Don't worry, bae. I'll protect you from the wildlife."

Celeste pantomimed kissing her biceps. "With your big guns?"

Throwing back his head, Ross laughed, the sound reverberating throughout the cab of the pickup. "I believe you're never going to let me live that down."

"You've got that right, because I'm going to remind you every time you get a little too cocky."

"It's not cockiness."

"What would you call it?"

"Confidence, Celeste. I've set goals for myself and worked hard to achieve them. I know who I am. What I want. And what I don't want. Geoff has always been my idol and as a kid I'd follow him everywhere and mimic everything he did. When he'd decided he wanted to join the rodeo it became a no-brainer for me. As a bronc rider, Geoff always made it look easy, and even though I pushed myself to extreme limits, I knew I would never be as good as him, so that's when I had to accept me for me."

"Are you saying that you like who you are and what you've become?"

"I like you, Celeste," he said, ignoring her question. "There isn't anything about you I don't like."

"This is not about me, Ross."

He decelerated to less than ten miles an hour. "Yes, it is. Every decision I make is about you. Everything I do is about you, until you tell me it's over."

Celeste could hardly believe the words.

"Are you trying to mess with my head, Ross?"

He gave her a quick glance. "No. You think telling you that I like you is messing with your head. I didn't freak out when you told me you liked me more than you should. You must make up your mind, Celeste."

"What about, Ross?"

"Whether you want to consummate our marriage."

"No," she said quickly. Celeste knew once they crossed that line there would be no turning back.

At least not for her.

Having sex would signal a commitment.

It would be for her and not Ross, because he'd said, *"There's much too much drama in committed relationships."* And he'd had enough drama with the online attacks on his character, while Celeste did not want to become a casualty once Ross grew tired of a wife he didn't love. He liked her, she turned him on sexually, but liking and sex wasn't enough. For Celeste it had to be love or nothing.

Ross came to a stop near the pasture where the horses were grazing. "I'm glad we agree because consummating our marriage would complicate everything."

Celeste managed to push all thoughts of their conversation to the farthest recesses of her mind when she walked over to the fence. One of the foals came over to nudge her with his nose. Reaching out, she stroked his head.

"Hi, beautiful. You seem to have grown since I last saw you. Mama's milk must be doing a body good." Domino snorted and shook her head. "You don't like her milk?" Domino shook her head again.

"Please don't tell me that you're able to speak to animals like Doctor Doolittle."

Celeste smiled at Ross. "Oh, you didn't know that I have special powers."

Resting his arms on the top rail, Ross chuckled. "No, but you certainly missed your calling."

"Why would you say that?"

Turning around, Ross gave her a direct stare. "You should've gone into veterinary medicine because you're able to easily connect with animals. First Scamp and now Domino."

"That's because I like animals, Ross. In fact, there are times when I like them better than human beings. They're loyal and unpretentious. And they never lie."

"That's because they can't talk."

Celeste ran her fingertips under the foal's chin. "They have their own way of communicating. Don't you, baby girl?" Domino snorted, then turned and trotted back to her mother. "How old are the foals?"

"They just turned two months. However, Traveler is a couple of weeks older than Domino."

"Commander was a busy boy impregnating two mares at the same time."

"The former owners weren't aware that both mares had come into estrus at the same time because they would've kept one of them separated from the stallion."

Celeste stared at Ross's profile. She'd noticed he rarely ventured outdoors without his Stetson. "Why would they want to do that?"

"Owning horses is an expensive undertaking, and they were saving money because they planned to live overseas. Even though a foal will suckle its mother until it's about six months old, beginning around the third month the mare's milk supply gradually decreases and a natural weaning process begins. It costs on average four to five thousand dollars a year to care for a healthy horse."

"Don't forget to include Scamp in that equation."

Ross opened his mouth to remind Celeste that Scamp was now her dog and once she went back to Chicago, he would accompany her, and she would be responsible for feeding him and paying his vet bills. Initially he'd felt the stray was a bother, sneaking in and out of the stables, but since he'd become a house pet, Ross had grown attached to the now overly affectionate puppy.

"Now that Scamp has a real home, he's become a couch potato. Don't look at me like that, sweetheart. I know he's been hanging out in the family room cuddling on the sofa or love seat with a certain person who has taken over the space as her office."

"He's just a puppy, Ross, and he needs to feel that he's loved."

Scamp isn't the only one who needs to feel that he's loved. Ross knew Celeste liked him—a lot—but he wanted her to love him as much as he was beginning to love her. He'd attempted to tell her how he felt without coming on too strong, but so far, he hadn't gotten his message across to her.

I like you, Celeste Burris.

I like you a lot.

More than I've ever liked any other woman.

No, I take that back. I've fallen in love with you.

Hell, you're my wife and I've taken a vow to love, protect, and care for you in sickness and in health as long as we both shall live. And I hope that's for a long, long time.

Ross couldn't utter the words. Ironic for a man who had always been unequivocally candid with other women. He'd told them he didn't do relationships or commitments. That he'd wanted to live his life by his leave, coming and going on his terms. He'd had only one serious relationship and it had been fraught with frantic telephone calls from a woman demanding to know where he was and when he was coming back. Initially he enjoyed the attention, but after a while her clinginess had begun to wear on him mentally and his performances took a hit. Geoff, who had noticed he was off his game, took him aside and demanded Ross tell him what was going on in his life outside the rodeo arena. Ross divulged everything and Geoff told him to take some time off competing to straighten out his personal life, but knowing he wasn't going to travel and compete with his brothers was a nonstarter. It had been the last time he got seriously involved with a woman. From then on, Ross Burris didn't do commitments.

But what else was his marriage to Celeste but a commitment? They were married, living together, and did things together most normal married couples did. Except consummate their union.

"Have you thought about breeding horses?"

At Celeste's question Ross shook off his thoughts. "I have more than enough on my plate to think about breeding horses. I'll leave that to Daniel Dubois. He's got a horse farm in Bronco Heights. His wife Brittany is Stephanie's sister."

Celeste laughed. "What did I say about needing a score card to identify who's who in your extended family?"

"There aren't that many branches on the family tree." Ross wanted to tell Celeste that the Montgomerys would occupy another branch if their brief marriage wasn't scheduled to end in divorce.

He saw the direction of Celeste's gaze and turned to see Jeremy walking toward them. Although he'd offered to pick Jeremy up and drive him back to Bronco, the former army medic had insisted he would call someone else. Ross suspected Jeremy felt he was a bother when it was the furthest from the truth.

"What's up, Jeremy?"

"I came to thank you for taking me to Billings. My sister was able to bring me back. When she told her boss that I was at the VA hospital, he let her off early because he's also former military."

Ross nodded. "Jeremy, I'd like you to meet my wife, Celeste. Celeste, Jeremy Shepherd. Not only is he our neighbor, but he's also a local hero. Jeremy was awarded the Bronze Star after his last deployment."

Ideas rolled around in Celeste's head like balls in a bingo drum when Ross mentioned that Jeremy was a hero. During the brief time she'd been in Bronco she'd encountered a number of high-profile personalities she'd categorized as larger-than-life, and her husband was among them.

Celeste flashed a friendly smile. "It's an honor to meet you. I don't know if Ross told you, but I'm a television reporter who's doing a piece on Bronco and I would love to interview you. I've already interviewed and submitted one on Mayor Smith, and I'd love to add you to my list."

"There's not much to tell, ma'am."

"Please call me Celeste, and if you don't mind, I'd like to be the judge of that. And I happen to know that the Bronze Star is awarded for heroic or meritorious achievement of service."

Jeremy pushed his tattered baseball cap off his forehead. "You seem to know a lot about the military."

"My brother is a JAG officer, and his wife is a military doctor."

Jeremy scratched his hair before pulling down his cap. "I supposed you'll know what questions to ask me."

"Instead of me asking the questions, Jeremy, I'm planning to let you do the talking."

"You would do that?" he asked.

"Of course. How's next week?" She was scheduled to talk to Brynn in two days, then she and Ross had plans for date night. "You can tell Ross when you're available and we'll set up a time and place to meet."

Jeremy smiled for the first time. "That sounds good. Maybe I can come over after Ross puts the horses out in the morning."

"If you come around seven you can eat breakfast with us."

"Thank you, ma'am. Ross, do you want me to put the horses in the stable?"

Ross nodded. "We can do it together."

Dean had raved to Celeste about her interview with Rafferty Smith, but it was the Places and Spaces correspondent who'd wanted more coverage on Bronco. She was going to make sure her segments on Ross, Jeremy, and Brynn would go over equally well.

Three hours later she sat on the floor in the family room in front of a roaring fire munching on freshly popped buttered popcorn and totally involved in an intense game of Scrabble with Ross. Scamp had found a spot a foot from the fireplace screen and flopped down to enjoy the warmth.

"That is not a word, Celeste. What the heck is *pusillani-mous*?" Ross questioned when she turned the Scrabble board to face him.

"It's an adjective that means lacking in courage or a coward. Just look it up."

"Nah, bae. I'm going to give you the benefit of the doubt and accept it. I just can't believe I'm married to a hustler."

Taking her cell phone off the sofa, she typed in the word and showed Ross the screen. "This should dispel some of your doubts."

"I believe you. It's a good thing we're not playing for money because I'd end up destitute."

"I wouldn't hustle you because you couldn't afford me," she countered, flashing a sexy grin.

"That depends on the stakes."

"What stakes?" she asked.

"Whatever it is you're willing to pony up."

"Oh no, you didn't go to the equine persuasion."

Ross winked at her. "Domino or the horses are not part of the deal."

"Have you forgotten I live in an apartment complex? So, horses are prohibited."

"Come on, Mrs. Burris. Stop stalling. Put up or shut up."

Celeste shook her head. She wasn't about to fall into that trap. She couldn't play along with Ross, because she did not trust herself not to blurt out her true feelings, and she could never tell him that he was so compelling, his virility so magnetic that he'd become a purely sensual banquet she wanted to devour.

If someone were to ask her what she really wanted she would have to say that she wanted to live in Bronco with her husband. That she would return to Chicago, check with HR, and submit her resignation. She knew she'd accrued enough vacation and personal days to cover the month of June until her contract expired.

Although Ross was aware their marriage was of short duration, he still hadn't told her outright that he wanted their marriage to extend beyond the thirty days. All he had to do was open his mouth and utter one little four-letter word—*stay*—and their lives and futures would change forever. They could consummate their marriage, sleep together every night, and shed the cloak of the charade that had begun to wear her down emotionally.

She wanted them to host dinner parties and invite friends and families into a home they'd made together. She wanted to volunteer to tutor students at his after-school center, and eventually for them to have children of their own.

It had taken only two weeks for her to think about not ordering from her favorite twenty-four-hour deli whenever she didn't feel like cooking for herself. It felt good not to concern herself about what to wear when she was scheduled to go on air or report from a remote location. And she'd become accustomed to not wearing makeup. Her complexion had improved and glowed with the appearance of natural good health, while a ponytail had replaced her previously professionally coiffed styles.

She had come to look forward to waking up to mountain views, inhaling clean air without the smell of exhaust from cars and buses, not hearing the ear-splitting wail of sirens from emergency vehicles, and gazing up at the clear nighttime sky littered with millions of stars that made her feel a part of Big Sky Country. Unconsciously she had morphed from a big city to a small-town girl who had fallen in love with her cowboy husband.

"I have nothing to put up," she said after a pregnant pause.

Ross shifted his position from facing Celeste to sitting next to her, draping an arm over her shoulders. "Yes, you do."

"What?"

"Ask your boss for an extension. Tell him you need more time to complete the assignment."

His idea sent Celeste's spirits soaring. He wanted her to stay longer. However, was longer just an extension? Would it be just another term limit—perhaps another thirty days to keep her hanging on with the hope it would become permanent?

"I doubt if he would approve it, Ross."

"Are you certain?"

She nodded. "Very certain. The NBA playoffs are in full gear, and I'm expected to report on some of the games. He's also scheduled me to cover some of the hockey playoff games."

"Do you ever get a break?"

"Yes. I usually take vacation in July or August."

"Bummer," he whispered.

Celeste wanted to tell him it didn't have to be a bummer if he would just acknowledge what they had was as close to perfect as it could get. And despite their no-sex rule, she enjoyed being married to Ross because of his easygoing personality. She woke each morning looking to share breakfast with Ross when they talked about their childhoods, national politics, and their favorite television show, *American Greed*. He chided her when she'd confessed to watching a marathon *Couples Court with the Cutlers*, claiming she would never get over her ex's duplicity if she continued to relive his cheating when viewing the episodes. She'd insisted the show was merely mindless entertainment.

Celeste never tired of going through his extensive collection of books stacked on shelves in one of the empty bedrooms. Ross claimed he planned to move them once he updated the house, but that would wait until the renovations to the building he'd purchased for his after-school program were completed. He'd shown her the blueprints for the structure, and he was scheduled to meet with the contractor before the end of the month to discuss costs. Whenever he talked about his plans for a life after the rodeo, she felt his excitement as surely as if it was her own.

Celeste rested her head on Ross's shoulder. "Do you want to finish this game or throw in the towel?"

"You really think I'm going to give up now because you think you're winning?"

"Think? You know I'm beating the pants off you."

"I thought we were playing Scrabble and not strip poker."

"You know that's not what I meant."

Ross pressed a kiss to her ear. "I'm a literal person, Celeste. I understand words to mean exactly what they say."

Celeste placed her hand at the middle of his back, enjoying the warmth of his body through his T-shirt. "Are you telling me I should monitor everything I say to you because it may be construed to mean something else?"

"Not everything. Just sexual innuendos because that would complicate what we'd agreed to."

Celeste dropped her hand. Just when she'd hoped beyond hope they could reach a point in their relationship when it could be more than a charade, she was reminded it was all a sham.

Although Ross wanted more time, Celeste knew it was impossible for her to continue the farce beyond the month. Every morning she woke in bed—alone—she knew nothing was going to change no matter how much she'd come to love him and how sexually frustrated she'd become.

"I don't know about you," she said, "but I'm ready to call it a night."

Ross kissed her ear. "Go to bed, sweetheart. I'll put everything away down here."

"Will you let Scamp out?"

"Yes, I'll take care of your baby."

Celeste pushed to her feet. "Good night, Ross."

"Good night and sleep well, sweetheart."

Sleep well. The two words nagged at Celeste as she climbed the staircase to her bedroom. She'd hoped to get a restful night's sleep because she needed to be strong enough to maintain control when she and Ross shared a bed when they spent the night at the Flying A ranch.

Chapter Fourteen

Celeste stared out the windshield watching the landscape change as Ross turned onto a stretch of road past a marker identifying the Flying A.

Celeste could not imagine growing up on a ranch and living there all her life. It would be like never leaving home. But she guessed things were different on Montana ranches. In rapid-fire succession, she asked questions about the spread before her.

Ross chuckled softly. "You're asking me a lot questions, sweetheart, when it's Garrett you should be asking."

Celeste was aware of the endearments that continued to flow so effortlessly off Ross's tongue. They appeared to be as normal for him as breathing. "It's Brynn I want to interview, not Garrett."

"You can't separate one from the other, Celeste. It's like interviewing a Burris and ignoring a Hawkins or a Brandt. Now that Brynn is engaged to marry an Abernathy, the Hawkinses have all become a part of the family dynamics."

"I'll never understand how all these couples got together."

Ross grunted and Celeste gave him a sidelong glance. "What was that all about?"

"The only thing I'm going to say is if you live here long enough, you'll become familiar with who's dating someone you'd never expect they would even give a passing glance to, not to mention the family rivalries and new money versus old money families."

"It sounds perfect," Celeste quipped.

"Yeah, for a reality show."

Celeste smiled. "There's that much drama, Ross?"

He chuckled, the sound rumbling in his chest. "As much or even more drama if folks discovered our real storyline."

She sobered. "There's no reason for anyone to find out about us if after I leave Bronco you don't inadvertently let the cat out of the bag."

Ross shook his head. "I won't tell if you don't."

"My lips are sealed."

"Mine, too, sweetheart."

There came whining from the rear seat and Celeste glanced over her shoulder to see Scamp in his pet carrier. Garrett had suggested bringing the puppy. "Do you think Scamp will get along with Garrett's dog?"

"We'll find out soon enough."

Celeste couldn't believe how quickly she and the puppy had bonded. When he wasn't sleeping in his kennel, he followed her in and out of every room in the house. He'd attempted to climb the staircase and fell twice before the third time was the charm. He'd made it to the top and was waiting for her when she went upstairs to gather the laundry. Doing laundry in Bronco was a lot easier than Chicago since she didn't have to schedule it around six other tenants.

Ross drove past a large building in the distance. "What's that building?" she asked.

"Abernathy Meats."

"They have a meat market on the property?"

"Yes."

"How many more surprises will I encounter before I leave Bronco?" Celeste said, under her breath.

"I don't know, bae. Only you can be the judge of that. Coming up on your right is the Abernathy family compound."

She stared with wide eyes at the sprawling house that would

take up at least half of a city block. When Ross had taken her to Doug's and introduced her to Garrett Abernathy, there was nothing in his demeanor or dress that indicated he came from wealth. Denim, flannel, Western boots, and hats were the norm for everyone, whether from Bronco Heights or Bronco Valley.

I could live and grow old here, because this is the first time in my life, I've ever felt this relaxed. Celeste forgot about Dean pressuring her at the station. As she looked out at the natural beauty of the Montana landscape, she suddenly wanted to see bison up close and ride a horse. But, she reminded herself, once she completed her piece on Ross and the others, it would be time to return to Chicago and life as she'd known it. Before she'd flown to Billings, Montana, unaware she'd come face-to-face with Ross Burris and marry him three days later.

Celeste exhaled an audible sigh as she closed her eyes. She'd known there was something very special about Ross when he leaned over the table to say, "You're so special that I couldn't imagine my life without you." There was so much passion and intensity in his eyes and in the words that she'd believed him. Or maybe it had been wishful thinking, that this incredibly handsome and übercharming man believed she would be perfect to step into the role as his temporary wife. So far, they'd been able to fool not only his friends, but more importantly the Burris family. Though Celeste continued to believe that Jeanne Burris had her doubts about them.

There was a saying that only two could keep a secret if one were dead. She didn't have to die for Ross to keep the secret. She would just have to leave Bronco, file for divorce, and never return.

"Garrett's house is coming up in another half mile."

Ross's deep, sensual voice shattered her thoughts as she shifted her attention back to the road ahead.

Ross drove past a log cabin off in the distance before turning down another paved road and maneuvering into the driveway of a large log-and-stone cabin built on a bluff with views of the mountains. The front door opened at the same time he shut off the engine, and Celeste smiled when Brynn came out of the house to meet them. A furry chocolate and white border collie appeared and stood next to Brynn.

She opened the rear door and reached for the pet carrier, while Ross retrieved their overnight bags. When she'd packed for the weekender earlier that morning Celeste did not dwell on the fact that she would have to share a bed with Ross, but now the reality charged her full force. She felt a flush she hoped didn't show on her face. She had no choice but to go through with it or risk their sham marriage being exposed. If that happened, there was no doubt she would be fired and never be able to get hired at another network. She'd not only be exposed as a liar but unethical.

Brynn came over and pointed to the carrier. "Look at this cute little puppy."

"I know you told me to bring him, but are you certain he'll get along with your dog?"

"Don't worry about Max. Since I've moved in, he's become a mush. Come into the house and I'll show you your bedroom."

Celeste followed Brynn into the great room with a cathedral ceiling and a wall of stone with a wood-burning fireplace. A curving staircase led to a second story catwalk that overlooked the leather sectional seating. Area rugs in muted shades of brown, tan, and gold enriched the coziness of the expansive space.

"I'm putting you and Ross in the bedroom down the hallway opposite ours. That way you can sleep in as late as you want and not be disturbed when Garrett gets up around five to take care of some of the chores around the ranch."

"Is Garrett working now?"

"No. He's in the back setting up the grill. I know it's only fifty degrees, but Garrett grills year-round. I don't complain because then we rarely have to clean up the kitchen after we cook."

Having grown up in Buffalo where some winters dropped a total of sixty feet of snow, Celeste couldn't believe anyone would grill in winter. She wondered if Ross was into what she jokingly called an extreme cookout. Not that she'd ever find out. She'd be long gone by winter. The closer the day of reckoning, the more she'd come to accept the reality that Ross and Bronco would eventually become events in the rearview mirror of her life, like so many others.

Celeste walked into the bedroom and the only object in the room she saw was the bed. She didn't know why, but she'd hoped for a king-size mattress so she would be able to scoot over to the edge and not contact Ross's hard body. Now, as she looked at the queen-size bed, she sent up a silent prayer that she would be able to survive the night without experiencing another one of her erotic dreams and begging her husband to make love to her.

"It's lovely, Brynn." The bedroom was beautifully furnished with solid oak furniture and linens in soft blues and greens which afforded it a Zen vibe. Floor-to-ceiling windows allowed for panoramic views of the mountains.

"You get settled and relax tonight. We'll do the interview tomorrow morning after breakfast, okay?" Brynn asked her. "Do you plan to videotape me?"

"I would like to if it's okay with you. I have the videographer on call from the convention center to tape my interviews. In fact, he taped my interview with Ross yesterday."

"Girl, I don't think I'd ever be able to pull that off. Asking Garrett questions, and if he chooses not to answer then gives me the death stare." She shook her head, her curls moving as if they'd taken on a life of their own. "Nope. I'm not willing to risk that."

Celeste wanted to tell Brynn that as a professional journalist she had to be impartial when interviewing a subject. That her personal views were just that. Personal. And at no time would she permit herself to be coerced or pulled into a situation where what she felt wasn't apparent. All she wanted were facts and the truth. Facts she could follow up on and authenticate.

"I'm going downstairs to check on the chef," Brynn said. "Come down whenever you're ready."

Celeste checked out the ensuite bath and walked back into the bedroom at the same time Ross entered, carrying their bags.

"Max and Scamp are best buds, and we should make arrangements with Garrett and Brynn for them to have a playdate."

"They're dogs, not children, Ross."

Ross set their bags at the foot of the bed. "But don't you call Scamp your baby boy?"

Celeste rested her hands at her waist. "That's just a figure of speech. Better yet, an endearment."

"Like *sweetheart* or *my love*." He gave her a direct stare. "Which one are you, Celeste? Sweetheart or my love?"

"Neither, Ross." She reached down for her suitcase, but he stepped in to grab it, their hands touching and their heads inches apart. She felt his breath on her cheek and dared to look at him. When would she ever get over marveling at how handsome he was?

Ross gave her one of his killer smiles. "Are you going to be all right sleeping in that bed with me?"

Ross had no idea she'd asked herself the same question over and over ever since Brynn had invited them to sleep over. She'd kept reminding herself that they had already shared a bed—the night she'd driven him home from Doug's, undressed him, and then got into bed with him until he fell asleep. However, that was then when he'd downed too many shots, and this was now when Ross was in total control of himself.

"Of course," she said, with more confidence than she felt at that moment. "Piece of cake."

"Wrong choice of words, sweetheart, because cake happens to be my favorite dessert, and I could eat it every night."

"Wasn't it you that said sexual innuendos will complicate things, Ross?"

Smiling, he shook his head. "I didn't mean it in a sexual way, so it's you who has sex on your mind."

There was no way Celeste was going to admit that she not only had sex on her mind but on her brain like a permanent tattoo and that she'd continually lusted after her husband in a way a wife should.

"I apologize if I gave off that impression," she said, instead.

Several seconds passed before Ross said, "Apology accepted."

Celeste didn't believe him, but decided not to press the point because she didn't want him to think she was protesting too much. "I'll be down in a minute. I want to put on a sweatshirt."

Ross dipped his head and kissed her forehead. "Do you want me to wait for you?"

"No, thanks. I won't be long."

She waited for Ross to leave before she returned to the bathroom to splash cool water on her face. The images of the bed and Ross standing much too close where she could feel his body heat, inhale his masculine cologne, and see the look in his eyes brought waves of heat from her head to the soles of her feet. Celeste knew she had to dig deep to regain a modicum of her tattered self-control, because with each sunrise it was becoming more and more difficult to conceal her feelings for Ross.

Celeste had acknowledged that she was attracted to Ross within minutes of meeting him, but what she did not understand was how her feelings had gone from liking to loving him in what she'd thought of as 1.2 seconds. And that had complicated everything.

Why did she have to go and fall in love with her husband when she knew it would lead to heartache once they broke up? From then on, she knew without question that every man she'd meet she would compare to Ross.

What she needed was a break. Once the month was up, she'd take some time off and go to a health spa in the desert to relax, rejuvenate, meditate so she could regain her mental and emotional equilibrium.

Celeste emerged from the ensuite bathroom to find Ross wearing a pair of pajamas pants as he stood, with his back to the windows, muscular arms crossed over his bare chest.

She had suggested he use the bathroom first because she'd hoped if she lingered long enough, he would be in bed—asleep. "You're still up."

Ross nodded. "I was waiting for you."

She took off her robe, placed it on a chair as she felt the heat of Ross's gaze with the motion. Although she had packed what she considered her least revealing nightgown it still wasn't enough because the light coming from the bedside table lamps illuminated her husband's bold stare. Her heart jolted as heat swept over her body from her face to her feet. Celeste felt as if she had been stripped naked as she found herself caught in a spell from which she did not want to escape.

Celeste knew this encounter would differ from when he'd asked her to stay with him, and when he'd lay beside her after her crying jag. In that instant she wished she could turn back the clock where the mention of sex hadn't become a part of their agreement. Her lips parted when he came closer, and she mumbled a silent prayer that she would be able to survive the night without begging her husband to make love to her.

Smiling, Ross cradled her face in his hands. He dipped his head and brushed a light kiss over Celeste's parted lips. Never had he wanted someone so much as he did at that moment. And it wasn't about sex. It was about living with and loving a woman who had come into his life when he'd least expected. A woman with whom he'd suggested they marry to advance her career and fix his image problem. But little did he know their marriage of convenience had become all too real for him. He released her face and pressed a kiss under her ear, inhaling the sensual scent of flowers on her silken skin.

"Let's go to bed, sweetheart." Taking her hand, he led her to the bed and waited for her to get in before slipping in beside her. Ross waited for Celeste to turn off her lamp, then reached over and turned off his. Once he heard her soft breathing, he knew Celeste had fallen asleep. This time their sleeping together had nothing to do with whether he'd had too much to drink or his comforting her because she was upset. It was because as newlyweds they were expected to share a bed.

Ross realized Celeste hadn't been completely truthful with him when she admitted she did not have a problem sharing a bed with him. They'd lived together long enough for him to know something about the woman he'd married. He'd found himself studying her when her attention was focused elsewhere. He knew when she was at peace when she lay on the chaise, eyes closed, with Scamp against her side.

Then there was the intensity in her expression when hunched over her laptop inputting notes or revising what she'd written.

Her annoyance was evident whenever she spoke to her boss, her responses polite but short and curt.

But it was when they interacted with each other, sitting, or standing close enough together for him to feel the whisper of her breath, smell the perfume that was so much a part of her femininity that he heard the increase in her respiration, saw the rapidly beating pulse in her throat, and how she failed to meet his eyes.

There was no doubt he'd made her uncomfortable and he hoped it was because everything about her made him feel uncomfortable but for the good. And the discomfort made Ross even more aware that his feelings for his wife had gone from mere liking to loving. There was nothing about Celeste he didn't love because she unknowingly had become what he needed to feel completely grounded and at peace with himself. He was able to feel her presence even if they weren't in the same room. She was beautiful, intelligent, independent, confident, and ambitious—all the traits he'd admired in a woman.

Ross wasn't certain if Celeste was happy being married to him, but he could honestly say that he was happy knowing she was in his life. But the time was fast approaching when she would be gone and that was something he did not want to accept. However, there was nothing he could do to stop her. She was leaving at the end of the month and never coming back.

Ross knew if he didn't try to get some sleep, he would be less than alert when he got up to go out with Garrett to get an up-front and personal view of a working ranch. Shifting to face Celeste's back, he draped an arm over her waist and waited for some of his anxiety to wane before he relaxed enough to fall asleep.

He normally slept in the buff, but in deference to Celeste he'd elected to pull on a pair of pajama pants, while she wore a cotton gown with a high neckline and long sleeves. It was the opposite of the lacy nightgown she'd chosen to wear on their wedding night—a night when he should have been able to have sex with his bride. Ross knew it would have been sex rather than lovemaking because at the time even though he'd been intensely attracted to Celeste he hadn't been in love with her. Fast-forward weeks later, he found himself loving her with a passion that made him crazy.

Ross wished they'd had a written rather than oral agreement that he could've ripped up. He'd wanted to confide in Garrett about the details of his marriage, because he suspected the rancher wouldn't judge him. But he knew it would be different with his family, especially his mother because she would never be able to trust him again. Neither would Celeste. It would devastate her if anyone were to know they'd concocted a deceitful plan.

He managed to fall asleep and when his internal clock woke him just before dawn, it was to find Celeste sprawled over his chest, sleeping soundly. Sometime during the night she'd shifted positions and climbed half on, and half off him. Ross felt the soft crush of her breasts and the strands of her unbound hair tickling his nose. He swallowed a groan when his body reacted to her scent, hopeless to stop his growing erection.

Ross knew he had to get Celeste off him, get out of bed. He managed to move her with a minimum of effort and slipped out of bed without waking her. He made it to the bathroom, closed the door, stepped into the shower, and turned on the water. As cold as he could make it. He stood under the spray until he was once more in control of his body.

Never again.

It was the first and the very last time he would share a bed with Celeste. It wasn't a promise, but a vow.

Celeste experienced exhilaration the first time she sat on a horse as she followed Brynn out of the stable to an open pasture where she was able to see the bison. As they rode, slowly and side by side, she took in the surrounding landscape.

Ross was up and out of the house by the time she woke and after showering and putting on her clothes she found Brynn in the kitchen gathering the ingredients to make breakfast. Brynn told her it was the perfect time to conduct the interview because Garrett had sent her a text that he and Ross would be back late because a calf had wandered off and got his leg tangled in barbed wire and they were driving the animal to the animal hospital.

After a breakfast with waffles, sausage links and coffee, Celeste called the videographer, asking him to come to the Flying A for the interview after Brynn told her about her grandmother Hattie Hawkins who'd lost her husband in a tragic rodeo accident shortly after their marriage and because she'd spent her childbearing years on the road she'd decided to adopt. She'd adopted Brynn's mother, Josie, and Hollie who are Black and two other daughters who are white and Latina. Hattie had adopted the girls as teenagers and taught them everything to know about performing, and they traveled the rodeo circuit as the original Hawkins Sisters.

During the interview she'd posed a question to Brynn. "I know men can earn a lot of money as rodeo riders, but was it the same for women?"

Brynn had shaken her head and stated, "While men could earn upward to a million dollars a year women earned a lot less because there weren't as many events as possible in which we could compete." She had also said, "Women rodeo performers are governed by strict rules around certain events, and because of this there has been a decrease in the number of women's rodeos in the last decade of the twentieth century because the cost of transporting a horse hundreds of miles to compete for the small purses the organization offered has become economically impractical. It is vastly different from the men's events because stock contractors supply the rodeos with bucking bulls, roping steers, and calves."

Once the interview concluded Celeste told Brynn she'd planned to contact the Professional Rodeo Cowboys Association for footage depicting women rodeo performers.

During the ride, Celeste thought about what Brynn had told her and she was constantly reminded that women earned a lot less than men for the same job; if or when she was promoted to chief sports correspondent, she doubted whether her increase in salary would be at least half of the current one.

Brynn laughed at her reaction when she saw the bison grazing off in the distance. "Close your mouth, Celeste."

"The babies are so adorable." Some were suckling their mothers.

Brynn nodded as she leaned on her saddle's horn. "The herd is growing."

"Is there enough grazing land on the ranch to sustain herds of cattle and bison?"

"Yes. With all their ranches, the Abernathys own hundreds of thousands of acres."

"And when you marry Garrett, you'll become another Abernathy."

"Don't play yourself, Celeste. Everyone in Bronco and probably Montana recognizes the Burris name. And after a while you won't be able to go anywhere in town with any shred of anonymity."

Celeste wanted to tell Brynn that she doubted that because in a couple of weeks she'd be packing her bags and leaving Bronco forever.

Brynn's cell phone pinged, and she took it out of her jacket to look at it. "Our men are back."

The women rode back to the stable and when Celeste got off the horse, she felt tightness in the muscles between her thighs and knew it would take time for her body to adapt to riding. Brynn drove them back to the house and stopped at a shed built under a large tree.

"This is where the magic happens," she said cryptically as she opened the door to a space filled with bins of yarn, bolts of fabric, and notions for her needlecraft enterprise. "I still plan to open a shop in Bronco Valley, but I want to wait until I have enough inventory to stock it."

Celeste stared in awe at the quilts, knitted and crocheted

garments, and wreaths depicting different seasons and holidays. "This is truly a magic workshop."

"I love working here. I'm here most days, except for Saturday and Sunday. They're what Garrett and I call family days. Either we'll spend the entire weekend together or visit family."

Celeste envied Brynn because in between competing with her sisters, she'd planned out her future, one she'd intimated would include starting a family once she and Garrett were married. It was as if the Hawkinses and Burrises had their lives on track while hers was going off the rails.

She decided to accelerate her schedule to finish her assignment sooner rather than later. Before she found herself so deep with Ross that she wouldn't be able to climb out.

Chapter Fifteen

Ross stared at Celeste across the table at Coeur de l'Ouest unable to believe she was able to improve on perfection. She'd looked beautiful to him every day, but tonight…

When she'd emerged from her bedroom Ross had felt weak in the knees, staring mutely at the black off-the-shoulder dress clinging to the curves of her slender body. He knew he had been gawking, but he couldn't help it when seeing her shapely legs in the sling strap stilettos that added four inches to her height. Then there was her hair. It was riot of tiny curls framing her face and falling to her bare shoulders that had him reacting like a starstruck teenage boy seeing his favorite actress in person. He hadn't been able to move or speak.

Ross thought her ethereal at their wedding, but tonight she radiated a sensuality that had humbled him because he could claim her as his wife. "I know I said it before, but you are so beautiful that I can't take my eyes off you."

Smiling, Celeste lowered her eyes and looked up at him through her lashes. "Didn't we talk about the effect on me of too many compliments?"

"It's the effect on me that I'm concerned about right now. Good thing I'm/sitting, or I'd surely embarrass myself."

"Stop it, Ross," she whispered.

"What if I don't want to or can't stop it, Celeste? There are just so many cold showers a man can endure before losing his mind."

* * *

Celeste frowned at her husband, resplendent in a dark tailored suit, white shirt, and navy-and-gold-striped silk tie. "Are you trying to ruin a perfectly good evening because you can't get your way?"

They'd returned from the Flying A Friday night and she'd insisted Ross review the interview because she'd wanted to get it over with and go back to Chicago. When he'd asked what the rush was, she blamed it on Dean.

She knew Ross wasn't happy, and it showed when he'd sat for the videotaping. What he hadn't realized was that his brooding expression made him appear serious and sensual at the same time. The interview took forty minutes and he had refused to watch the playback. He merely signed the release and stalked out of the house.

The little black dress she'd chosen to wear achieved the reaction she sought because she wanted to remind Ross of what he was going to miss in a couple of days. She'd planned to leave Bronco within a few days after meeting with Jeremy because there was no other reason to stay. She did not want to prolong the inevitable.

A scowl distorted his handsome features. "And what way is that?" he asked, between clenched teeth.

"I'd rather not say. We can discuss this when we get home." She sat back in her chair when she noticed his demeanor soften.

"Good, because I want this night to be special."

Celeste smiled. "And it is, because it's date night and it's very different from our last one."

Ross's smile matched hers. "You're right because doing shots here isn't the norm."

"I really like this place."

"I figured you would because it's bougie just like you. I knew you'd fit in well here. You should do lunch at The Association. It's a private club for wealthy ranchers."

Celeste bristled. "Why do I get the impression that you're insulting me, Ross?"

"No. I'm just stating a fact."

"Are you saying I should've hooked up with a Taylor or an Abernathy rather than a Burris?"

Ross couldn't believe it. He'd attempted to pay Celeste a compliment and ended up putting his boot in his mouth. "No, sweetheart," he hurried to say as he took her hand in his, "you married who you were supposed to marry. And I'm sorry if you believe I insulted you. You must accept that you're an elegant woman and I'm happier than a pig in slop that you're married to me."

"Do you realize that you do a lot of apologizing?"

"That's because I still don't know who Celeste Burris is, and I doubt if I'll know her fully even if we get to spend the rest of our lives together."

"I'm not that complicated. What you see is what you get."

His eyebrows lifted. "And I like what I see—a lot."

"Ditto."

The waiter approached the table to take their beverage and dining selections and offered Ross a reprieve. He realized he was coming off as testy because time was growing close when Celeste would leave, and he didn't want her to leave, but knew there was nothing he could do about it.

He'd begun sleeping less and staying away from the house for longer periods of time. He'd met with the architect who'd updated the plans for his student center. And when he'd sat for the interview with Celeste, he'd spent more time talking about his after-school enrichment program than his career in rodeo. And because she hadn't prepped him in advance Ross had to pause before answering some of the questions, especially ones about the comments posted about him on social media platforms. He'd answered as truthfully as he could and thankfully, she segued to another topic.

He'd stopped to see his mother and when Jeanne asked about Celeste, he was forthcoming when he told her about the assignments she had to complete before going back to Chicago. Jeanne admitted he'd chosen well and asked him to bring his wife by to see her again once she returned to Bronco, hopefully to stay. Ross couldn't tell his mother that wasn't going to happen and said he would relay the message to Celeste.

Dinner was perfect once Ross decided to stop agonizing over Celeste leaving and instead to savor the time they had left. He'd ordered a bottle of champagne and Celeste held up two fingers indicating two glasses was her limit. He stared at her when she opened her evening bag to take out her phone.

"I just got a text from Jeremy saying he was sorry, but he'd decided not to be interviewed about his time in the military because there were incidents he was trying to forget."

"What did you tell him?"

"I said it was okay because I understand why he wouldn't want to talk about it."

"I didn't want to tell Jeremy's business but he's suffering from PTSD." Celeste nodded. "I hope Jeremy will get the help he needs, but I don't know if that's possible when he has to go to Billings to see VA doctors."

"Aren't there therapists in Bronco?" Celeste questioned.

"Yes, but he has to be willing to be seen by them."

Celeste took a sip from her flute. "Hopefully one of these days when I come back to Bronco for a visit and to catch up on old times he'll be better."

"Is that really what you want, Celeste? To come back to Bronco when now you can't wait to leave?"

"I need to go back and finish my assignments."

"Will you stay if you're promoted?"

Celeste wanted to tell Ross that was a question she'd asked herself over and over and was unable to answer. "I don't know, Ross. I suppose I'll just have to wait and see."

Her entire life had taken on wait status the day Dean called her into his office to tell her he was sending her to Bronco to interview Geoff Burris. When she'd told him she hadn't heard of Geoff Burris and had no idea where Bronco was, he'd unceremoniously dismissed her with an order to research both because, as he said, "That's what journalists are trained to do."

Little did Dean know he was sending her off to fall in love with her husband and find a town that made her feel as if she truly had come home. She was now a big-city girl with small-town sensibilities.

"What are you smiling about?" Ross asked her.

"How comfortable I feel being in a small town."

"Being in one but not living in one. There's a difference."

She couldn't deny that. After all, she was leaving soon. "You're right."

Those were the two last words they exchanged as Celeste concentrated on her dinner while enjoying the most magnificent views she'd experienced since coming to Montana, and again she reminded herself that she could so easily get used to living in Big Sky Country.

The drive back to Bronco was completed in silence, each lost in their own private thoughts, and when Ross stopped the vehicle in front of the house, Celeste did not wait for him to assist her out, but removed the house key he'd given her and unlocked the door, not bothering to check on Scamp because Ross had assumed the responsibility of taking care of him at night.

She kicked off her shoes and headed for her bath to remove her makeup. She pulled her dress over her head and walked back into the bedroom, stopping when she saw Ross standing in the middle of the room. He'd taken off his suit jacket and tie and unbuttoned the collar to his shirt.

Celeste held her dress in front of her to keep him from seeing the black lacy strapless bra and matching bikini panties. "What do you want?"

"Once you leave, I don't want you to come back."

She went still. "What did you say?"

"You heard what I said, Celeste. Don't come back."

Her temper flared. She'd had enough with her boss issuing unreasonable demands, and now it was her fake husband. "Don't you ever tell me what I can and cannot do. In case you've forgotten I happened to be a grown-ass woman who will come and go as she pleases and—"

Celeste did not and could not recall Ross moving, but suddenly he took the dress from her grasp and slanted his mouth overs for a kiss that siphoned the air from her lungs. Rage and passion merged, and she found herself kissing him back as her fingernails dug into his back through the fabric of his shirt.

One moment she was standing, the next she was sprawled over the bed as Ross removed her bra and panties until she lay naked under him. He slipped off the bed and less than a minute later he, too, was naked and Celeste couldn't pull her eyes away from his magnificent body. He opened the drawer in the bedside table, searching until he found a condom, and Celeste watched as he slipped on the protection, desire burning in every part of her.

His mouth was everywhere. It was as if her body had become a dessert he sought to eat in tiny morsels until he devoured it all. By the time he'd buried his face between her legs, Celeste could not stop the screams locked in her throat. She felt as if she were slipping to a place she'd never been when he penetrated her in one sure thrust of his hips, and her screams became moans of ecstasy when she experienced for the first time what it truly meant to be made love to.

Ross took her on a journey of highs where she was close to climaxing, then he slowed, allowing her to float back to reality until he reignited the flames of passion that threatened to explode her into million pieces. When she could no longer hold back, she felt her body convulse as waves of pleasure took her higher until she surrendered all she was and would be to the man she would love forever. She and Ross climaxed together. She felt the runaway beating of his heart against her breasts, then his soft laughter in her ear. "You were more than I could've ever imagined."

Celeste smiled. "You were pretty good yourself."

He kissed her. "Does this mean you want seconds?"

"Yes."

Not only did she have seconds but also thirds and more. Celeste could not believe that they'd waited until it was almost time for her to leave to consummate their marriage, but she was glad they had.

Celeste discovered Ross was insatiable as they made love all night long, until exhaustion won out. She woke the next morning to find him in bed beside her. "Good morning."

He smiled. "That it is. People claim baby making and makeup sex is incredible, but for me breakup sex trumps the other two."

Celeste felt as if someone had poured a bucket of ice water over her. She didn't want to believe his making love to her was his way of saying goodbye. "Yes, it is. Thanks for the parting gift."

Ross pounded the mattress in his room. He didn't know why he'd said what he did, but it had come out all wrong. And it was too late to retract it. He'd retreated to his bedroom, gotten dressed, and now stood outside her bedroom door. When it opened, Celeste was fully dressed and pulling her suitcase behind her.

He felt as if someone had reached inside his chest to squeeze his heart until he struggled to breathe. He couldn't believe she was leaving before the thirty days were up. And something told him his wife was leaving and never coming back.

"I'll never forget you, Celeste." She shot him a death stare and if looks could kill he would've dropped dead on the spot. "I'll drive you to the airport."

"Don't bother," she snapped. "I have an Uber outside that will take me to the hotel to pick up my rental car."

Ross knew there was nothing he could do or say to change things. Celeste had said all along that she did not plan to stay in Bronco, and he'd believed he would be ready when the day came. But that was before he'd fallen in love with his temporary wife.

He watched her walk out, his tongue plastered to the roof of his mouth and his heart broken in two.

He went downstairs and saw Scamp staring at him. "She's gone, buddy. And I don't know what to do to get her back. Maybe we should give her time and maybe she'll change her mind. What do you think?" Scamp just lowered his head, walked into his kennel, and sat down. It was obvious the puppy knew she was not coming back.

It took Ross less than twenty-four hours to realize he couldn't stay in the house. It felt strange. Empty. Now he understood what his brothers were talking about when they said the right woman could make life complete. And for Ross, Celeste was that woman. But she was gone.

Celeste couldn't book a flight to Chicago until later that evening, so she passed the time in the terminal reading countless magazines and drinking endless cups of coffee to stay alert. It was foolish to leave for the airport without a reservation, but she couldn't have spent another moment with Ross. Not that she had anyone but herself to blame for her situation. She'd gone into their marriage with her eyes wide, knowing exactly how it would end. And she knew who the man she married was from the beginning. He'd never wanted commitment and that's why he proposed the month-long marriage.

And now, days before the month was over, she was the one to end it.

Her phone pinged a text from him, and she ignored it. Then he called and she also ignored it. There was nothing left to say to each other. She finally sent him a text telling him it was over, not to contact her again. They need to make a clean break.

Celeste walked into the newsroom after stopping at her apartment to shower and change her clothes and was met with applause. She was now the affiliate's new IT girl. Her colleagues' reaction wasn't as shocking as the news that Dean had been promoted, ironically because of the success of Celeste's work in Bronco.

Still, she told herself she was a winner because she didn't have to work with Dean. Even though she didn't have to deal with the toxic relationship she had experienced with Dean as her boss, Celeste now felt more comfortable at the station than she did at home. It was at home where she hadn't had the distractions, she needed to keep her mind off her husband. And yes, Ross Burris was still legally her husband, while she planned to wait two months before contacting a lawyer to file for a divorce from a man with whom she had fallen inexorably in love. Not only did she miss him, but she also missed Scamp, and Montana.

Job offers from several network affiliates poured in, but she wondered if they'd still want to hire her if they knew she'd split with her rodeo husband. Even worse if they uncovered their marriage was a farce and she was a fake.

She needed to get away. She put in for vacation, planning to use the time to assess whether she was going to stay at WWCH or…

She didn't need to think of the alternative because in her hearts of hearts she knew what she wanted. She wanted to go back to Bronco. And to her husband, despite the way things ended between them.

The minute she got home she went online and purchased a one-way ticket from Chicago to Billings, Montana. Ross hadn't attempted to contact her when she told him they had to make a clean break, but that no longer mattered. She was in love with her husband, and she had to find out if they could make a go of it.

She would return to Bronco and apply for a position at a Billings TV affiliate or write for the *Bronco Bulletin*. It didn't matter where she worked if she could go to bed and wake up beside her husband.

Ross sat on a chair in the family room as he listened to Geoff via Zoom go on and on about the countries he had visited during his European vacation. "I can't explain it, but I'm beginning to feel homesick," his brother admitted.

"I don't have to leave the country to hanker about coming back to Bronco," Ross said.

Geoff nodded. "I know what you mean. What about your wife, bro? When I spoke to Mom, she told me Celeste left Bronco for Chicago. Do you know when she's coming back?"

Sandwiching his hands between his knees, Ross stared at the pattern on the throw rug rather than his laptop. He knew he had to level with his brother before the truth was revealed. "She's not coming back."

A frown settled into Geoff's features. "What the hell do you mean she's not coming back?"

Ross felt a shiver of annoyance snake up his spine with his brother's tone. "We split up. End of story."

Geoff shook his head. "Something's not adding up, Ross. You marry the woman, live with her, now you're claiming it's all over.

"It's not that simple, Geoff." He wanted to tell his brother everything but knew it would sound even more preposterous that he had proposed marriage to a woman he'd just met. "We had a disagreement and she left."

Geoff ran a large hand over his face at the same time he shook his head. "I don't believe this. You and your wife had a disagreement and she walked out on you?"

"She was scheduled to return to Chicago once her assignment was completed," Ross said in defense of Celeste.

"To return to stay?" Geoff asked. Ross nodded. "Have you tried to contact her?"

Ross nodded again. "Yes, but she won't take my calls or my texts."

A beat passed before Geoff asked, "Do you love her?"

A swollen silence followed Geoff's query before Ross said, "With all my heart." The admission had come from somewhere he hadn't known existed. He loved Celeste enough to want to spend the rest of his life with her, but only if she would give him a second chance to prove it to her. He didn't want a thirty-day marriage but one that spanned more than thirty years.

As the eldest of Benjamin and Jeanne Burrises sons, Geoff had come to know his brothers well enough to know when something was bothering them, and judging from Ross's expression and body language he knew he was hurting. At first, he didn't want to believe that Ross had been seeing a woman in secret, and then decided to elope even before introducing her to the family. Although he hadn't met Celeste in person, he'd sensed there had to be something very special about her for Ross to give up his bachelor lifestyle to settle down with one woman.

"I don't believe," Geoff said, shaking his head, "that you would give up that easily. Burrises are competitors not quitters, Ross. You have one speed bump with your wife and now you cut and run. Relationships aren't easy. Stephanie and I have had our share of disagreements, but our love for each other is strong enough for us to stay together. He paused. "If you love Celeste, then you must be willing to fight for her, and I'm willing to help you out."

Ross's head popped up. "How?"

"It's one in the afternoon here in Rome, but it's early enough in the States for me to arrange for a plane to take you to O'Hare so you can tell your wife whatever you need to reconcile. And it wouldn't hurt to grovel a little bit."

Ross's eyebrows lifted slightly. "Grovel?"

Geoff smiled. "Yes, grovel. I can assure you that it works when you need it. Hang on while I reserve your flight," he said, reaching for his cell phone. Ten minutes later, Geoff said, "All set. You have three hours to make it to the Billings airport for your flight into O'Hare. Once you touchdown you're on your own, brother."

Ross smiled. "Thanks, bro. I supposed I needed a little prodding to see things differently."

"What you needed was a swift kick in the behind, but after being bucked off a few broncs over the years that probably wouldn't have had much of an impact on you."

Ross chuckled. He thanked Geoff again, logged off, and then called Jeremy to tell him to look after Scamp before he went up upstairs to pack.

Minutes after arriving at O'Hare Celeste heard someone calling her name. She turned to see Ross running toward her. "What are you doing here? I was just about to go through security."

"I came to see you."

Celeste's heart was beating so fast she feared hyperventilating. "Why?"

"Because I've been going crazy without you. I know staying together wasn't a part of our plan, but I think we belong together. If you come back to Bronco, I'll prove it to you."

Her eyelids fluttered wildly. "I can't believe this is happening. What made you change your mind?"

"I never changed my mind, sweetheart. I didn't lie when I told everyone I fell in love with you at first sight. It just took me awhile to prove it to myself."

Celeste shook her head. "This is too much for my heart to take in."

"Why?"

She handed him her ticket. "I was on my way to Bronco to see you."

"Well, you'd better put in for a refund because Geoff chartered a private jet to take us home."

"You told Geoff about us? Our temporary marriage?"

Cradling her face, Ross kissed her forehead. "No. Because I didn't lie when I told him that I was in love with you and couldn't imagine spending my life without you."

She smiled. "Well, husband, it was the same with me. I can't even remember when I realized I love you but it's enough to know you love me."

"We need to go to another terminal to board the jet. We'll only have a few days to make up for lost time because I'm scheduled to return to the circuit for a couple of weeks."

"Don't worry, I'll be at home waiting for you."

"You and Scamp. He also misses you. But you're really going to enjoy summer in Bronco. The Fourth of July celebration lasts almost an entire week."

"What about the fall and winter?"

"That's when you'll get to see the Mistletoe Rodeo and the Christmas tree lighting. Every season in Bronco is spectacular and what makes it even more special is that we'll get to experience all the seasons together from now on. What say you, Mrs. Burris?"

"I say yes, Mr. Burris." She wrapped her arms around his neck. "I love you, Ross."

He pulled her closer and kissed her. "I love you more."

She stayed wrapped in his arms as they made their way to the sleek private jet waiting to take them home.

Home to Bronco, Montana.

* * * * *